ENTERPRISE™

ENTERPRISE™

SHOCKWAVE

NOVELIZATION BY **PAUL RUDITIS**
WRITTEN BY **RICK BERMAN & BRANNON BRAGA**

BASED ON *STAR TREK*® CREATED BY **GENE RODDENBERRY**
AND *ENTERPRISE* CREATED BY **RICK BERMAN**
& BRANNON BRAGA

POCKET BOOKS
New York   London   Toronto   Sydney   Singapore

An *Original* Publication of POCKET BOOKS

POCKET BOOKS, a division of Simon & Schuster, Inc.
1230 Avenue of the Americas, New York, NY 10020

STAR TREK is a Registered Trademark of
Paramount Pictures.

This book is published by Pocket Books, a division of
Simon & Schuster, Inc., under exclusive license from
Paramount Pictures.

ISBN: 0-7434-6455-9

First Pocket Books printing October 2002

10   9   8   7   6   5   4   3   2   1

POCKET and colophon are registered trademarks of
Simon & Schuster, Inc.

For information regarding special discounts for bulk purchases,
please contact Simon & Schuster Special Sales at 1-800-456-6798 or
business@simonandschuster.com

Printed in the U.S.A.

Includes excerpts from the following episodes:

"Cold Front" written by Stephen Beck & Tim Finch
"Detained" teleplay by Mike Sussman & Phyllis Strong; story by Rick Berman &
Brannon Braga

For Chris Van Note-Burman

ENTERPRISE™

SHOCKWAVE

Prologue

"Next you have a briefing with the I.M.E." The lieutenant junior grade rattled off the list as they sped down the halls of Starfleet Headquarters. "From there you're meeting with Commander Williams on the Starfleet Headquarters expansion project, followed by a briefing concerning the Vulcan/Andorian situation, and then there's the ground-breaking for the newest Zefram Cochrane Elementary School. Since the school is in Australia, you'll be doing that one via comlink."

Admiral Forrest continued down the hall, moving at his now customary speed, which was twice the pace he used to walk before *Enterprise* started its mission ten months ago. *Why don't I ever just stroll places anymore?* he wondered, only halfheartedly listening to his schedule for the day. The itinerary never mattered this early in the morning, as it was bound to change a half dozen times before he even made it to his next destination. Checking the time,

Forrest noted that technically his workday wasn't even supposed to have begun yet and he was already running fifteen minutes late.

". . . Afterward you have a brief meet-and-greet scheduled with the newest group of cadets, and that brings us to lunch." The lieutenant looked as if he was already exhausted. Forrest had to give the kid credit. As keeper of the schedule, he was the first one in the office in the mornings and the last one out at night. Of course, most of the stress in the lieutenant's life came from the fact that he revered the schedule as if it were written on stone tablets as opposed to being a general *guide* to the day, merely *suggesting* things that the admiral was supposed to do.

"But you are going to allow me to have a lunch today, right? I mean more than just a ration pack on the go like the last two days." Forrest liked to tease the lieutenant about his schedule. Sometimes it was the only fun he had in a day.

"Certainly, sir," he replied, slightly flustered. "You have a lunch meeting with Ambassador Soval."

And sometimes the joke backfired.

"Very well." Forrest tried not to sound too frustrated by the meal plan. It was best to keep his personal feelings from his command staff in certain situations. It wasn't that Forrest held any particular animosity toward the Vulcan, he had just never managed to get through a meal with the ambassador without suffering indigestion.

"And that brings us to the afternoon schedule," the lieutenant continued.

They had finally reached Forrest's office. "We'll worry about that later," he said, halting. "I have some things to go over. Why don't you take a break?"

"Begging the admiral's pardon, but the I.M.E. briefing was scheduled to begin—"

"I know, Lieutenant," he interrupted. "But here's the best part about being admiral: no matter what time something is *scheduled* to begin, they're not going to start without me. Trust me, Lieutenant, the Interspecies Medical Exchange isn't going anywhere."

"Yes, sir." The lieutenant looked as if he was about to mark down that valuable piece of information in his copious notes.

"I'll just be a few minutes," Forrest assured him. "Why don't you go take a coffee break, or possibly something without caffeine."

"I actually have some work to do on your afternoon schedule, sir."

"I thought you might," Forrest mumbled, waiting for him to leave. "Dismissed."

"Yes, sir."

Entering his office, Admiral Forrest took a deep breath, wishing he had an hour to relax before he was expected to be in his next meeting. He had often hoped someone would finally perfect those transporting devices so that he could have one installed in his office and he could just beam himself from meeting to meeting. Until such a time, Forrest would have to settle for these little unplanned breaks to lighten the load. He stood, looking out the window at the San Francisco Bay, wishing that the damn window opened so he could at least get some fresh air.

Although there was a ton of work on his desk, he didn't really have anything pressing to look over contrary to what he had told his aide. He simply needed to take a few minutes for himself before the day began to overwhelm him right out of the starting gate. But as he stood looking out at the beautiful vista, the voice in the back of his head kept nagging at him that he should get to work.

Sitting behind his desk, he did a quick scan through his computer to make sure nothing important had come overnight. Pleasingly, he found nothing more than the usual memos and reports.

Never one to sit idly, even when relaxing, Forrest took a moment to look over the latest ship designs. If *Enterprise*'s mission continued to meet with the same success it had been seeing, he hoped that it wouldn't be long before they had an entire fleet of Warp Five ships deployed to explore the stars.

And all of them out there without you, he thought with a twinge of regret.

He couldn't help but envy the many varied and exciting experiences of the *Enterprise* crew. Granted, Archer's mission had hit its fair share of snags, but that was to be expected. However, no matter what the ultimate outcome, every day *Enterprise* was in space provided copious amounts of new information leading to the formation of additional departments for research, theoretical discussion, and, of course, meetings. They were on the verge of a new age, and like the Industrial and Technological ages before them, Forrest knew that this would be a time for great strides in the evolution of the human race.

And I get to oversee it all from behind a desk.

Every time Forrest had a briefing or just a simple conversation with Captain Archer, he would feel the stirrings of jealousy. To be out there, among the stars, exploring was something every member of Starfleet wished he or she could be doing, and Admiral Forrest had the unenviable position of being the one on the receiving end of all the new information. He got to be the one to see excitement on Archer's face and hear the lilt in his voice as the captain detailed one discovery after another. And, short of being out there himself, Forrest wouldn't have changed his position for the world.

The Vulcans made it known that they would have preferred Captain Gardner to lead the first exploratory team into what had previously been known as "deep space." But Forrest knew that Starfleet had made the right choice in Archer because the two shared an understanding of what it meant to be explorers, and that kinship made the admiral feel as if, in a way, he was out there as well.

"Admiral," his aide's voice came over the private comlink from the outer office.

With a heavy sigh, Forrest roused himself from his musings. "I'm on my way," he said before he could be reminded, once again, that there were people waiting to meet with him. What he had said before was true. The meeting certainly wouldn't begin without him, but there was only so long he could keep people from their jobs.

Pulling himself out of his chair, Forrest stopped for a moment and looked into the corner of his office, thinking it would be the perfect place to put one of those biotransport platforms. Stepping out of his office, he found his aide waiting with a padd, ready to go over the rest of the schedule.

This is going to be a long day.

Chapter 1

Enterprise sailed toward the planet at low warp, setting an almost leisurely pace in keeping with the mood of the crew. Even though only a portion of them had been able to take part in the recent shore leave on Risa—the self-proclaimed pleasure planet—the mood of relaxation had been contagious. Throughout the ship, people were considerably less stressed and actually appeared to be enjoying the often repetitive tasks of maintaining the ship as it traveled through space. Of course it helped that no one had fired upon the ship in several days.

In their current mission, making contact with a new species was primarily the responsibility of the senior staff, while the rest of the crew continued their day-to-day work, eagerly anticipating data regarding the latest alien interaction. Once the data began streaming in, their fun began. Each department would glean bits of information most suited to its field of study and then examine it, learn from it, and prepare a report. The reports would be logged, compiled, and forwarded to Starfleet, where the folks back home would have their own fun. Being on the front line of exploring new worlds and new civilizations made even the lowest ranking crewmembers beam with pride over the importance of even the most menial of jobs.

True, there had been some awkward first contacts, the Klingons and the Andorians came to mind. Despite his crew's best efforts, the Klingons had been downright hostile. The Andorians dubbed the humans "pinkskins" and judged them guilty by association, but they seemed to be thawing . . . a little. The same could not be said of the race that was humanity's very first alien encounter, the Vulcans.

Captain Jonathan Archer thought over those first contact situations as he walked through the corridors of *Enterprise*. Their next mission promised to be almost as relaxing as the recent R&R had been—or, he hoped, even more so considering his visit to Risa had ended rather abruptly.

Archer always looked forward to the thrill of making contact with new alien races even more than the rest of his crew did, although he tried not let it show through the professional air expected of all Starfleet captains. It was often difficult for him to keep in mind that with every thing he said and every move he made, he was representing the entire populace of Earth. It was daunting to say the least.

"Mornin', Captain," Commander Charles "Trip" Tucker said as he and Sub-Commander T'Pol caught up with Archer as they passed the mess hall.

"Sir." The Vulcan nodded her greeting.

"Good morning," he replied. "Have all the preparations been made?"

"Yes, sir," T'Pol replied. "We should be entering the star system shortly."

"They don't have a problem with us dropping by?" Archer asked as he entered his private mess followed by the officers. Stepping up to the serving station, he poured coffee for himself and Trip. Archer then poured T'Pol her mug of hot water and noted silently as she added a slice of lemon.

"Living dangerously?" teased Trip.

As the ranking officers on *Enterprise*, the trio had grown into a rather comfortable and sometimes even informal working relationship. Archer and Trip had been friends for years and quite often fell into casual banter when discussing official business. However, as a Vulcan, T'Pol had been much slower to understand the benefits of such a friendly, informal atmosphere, but had been gradually coming around as she grew more comfortable with the erratically emotional crew.

"On the contrary." T'Pol ignored Trip's teasing and continued her report. "The operations supervisor said they haven't had visitors in nearly six months."

A sly smile came to Trip's face. "Is it really a matriarchal society?" The grin broadened as his mind played over the full implications of his question. "Do the women make all the decisions?"

"Until recently," T'Pol explained, apparently without noticing the subtext in Trip's sudden interest in the colony's hierarchical structure. "But in the last decade, the Paraagan males have made great strides to acquire equal rights."

Accepting his own cup of coffee from the captain, Trip conspiratorially added under his breath, "Still, it'd probably be best if we didn't get too flirtatious."

"Probably," Archer agreed, knowing that the odds of his chief engineer making such a breech in protocol with the colony's leaders were slim, but probably higher than the possibility that *he* would do such. Back to the topic at hand, Archer was impressed by the accomplishments of the society they were about to visit. "I read that the colony started off twenty years ago with just thirty miners and now there are over three thousand. They have schools, landscaped communities, and even some kind of museum."

The three officers took their seats around the table, their empty breakfast plates waiting to be filled. They often dined together in the captain's mess, and their places had already been set for them as their meal was being prepared by Chef.

Trip considered the accomplishments of the Paraagans. "You think twenty years from now there'll be Earth colonies out this far? Human kids growing up on 'New Sausalito'?"

Archer thought over the idea while a flood of possibilities flashed through his mind. Their mission could easily involve discovering those suitable environments in which Earth could expand its borders into space. Early human exploration had always been motivated by the search for new land. Though Starfleet's interests were primarily scientific, it wasn't too much of a jump to add territorial concerns to the list.

"If my father was alive, he wouldn't doubt it for a minute," Archer said, referring to the man who had introduced him to the concept of space exploration, inspired his interests, and helped nurture them. "We're making history with . . ."

". . . with every light-year," Trip continued the sentiment in unison with his captain and friend. "You know, I think I've heard you say that at least half a dozen times."

Archer was a bit embarrassed at being caught in his inspired ramblings. He took an almost gleeful pride at being given the opportunity to live out his dream, and his father's as well. It certainly wasn't his fault that every now and then he was awestruck by the enormity of what his crew was doing. The first humans to travel so far out into space, visiting new planets. *How many other people woke up this morning to prepare for a meeting with a new race of people?*

The com chirped, rousing Archer from his thoughts. Getting up from his chair, he took a few steps to the companel on the wall and pressed a button to make contact with whoever was paging him. "Archer here," he said into the air.

"The Paraagans have given us clearance to enter orbit," Ensign Mayweather's voice came over the com system.

"Have you received their landing protocols?" T'Pol asked from her seat.

"They're coming in now," Mayweather confirmed.

"We're on our way," Archer replied.

Trip and T'Pol were immediately out of their chairs.

"I hate meeting new people on an empty stomach," Trip said, looking down at the still empty plates.

"Perhaps you can find a Paraagan male willing to prepare you a substantial meal," T'Pol suggested, implying that she hadn't entirely missed the sexist undertones of the earlier part of the conversation.

Archer enjoyed seeing Trip caught off guard by her comment. He remembered how difficult things had been when she was first assigned to join them on their mission to return the Klingon, Klaag, to his homeworld. With every passing day she seemed to be better ingratiating herself into the crew and even developing a rather dry sense of humor. That's not to say that the crew was entirely at ease with the Vulcan science officer, but things were definitely getting better. Archer felt that the close Vulcan/human interaction was having a positive effect on T'Pol. The way she regarded humans had changed dramatically since her first days on the ship.

In much the same way, Archer knew that she had been changing his opinion toward Vulcans on the whole. Her calm, steady manner often provided the stability he needed in extreme situations, and her mere presence on his ship helped him better understand some of the misconceptions he had concerning her race.

"So what kind of greeting should we expect from the Paraagans? Are there any ceremonial customs we need to be briefed on?" Archer asked as they made they way to the launch bay. The main level of the bay was up one deck, but they could get to the shuttlepod just as easily by going through the lower level on E-deck.

"While the Paraagans as a race do observe a number of ceremonial customs," T'Pol explained as they continued their way around the corridors in the outer rim of the deck, "the colony has eschewed some of those customs. Their society has developed more of a . . . nonconformist attitude."

"Sounds like my kind of people," Trip said.

"There are no ritual greetings to my knowledge," T'Pol concluded, ignoring that last comment.

Archer nodded to a passing crewman. "You know, we should really consider bringing some kind of gift from Starfleet in these situations. We might want to design some kind of commemorative souvenir that is indicative of Earth culture."

"How 'bout one of them night-lights in the shape of Zefram Cochrane they sell in the gift shops in the Embarcadero," Trip suggested with a laugh. "Kids just love those things."

Archer chuckled at the idea as well, knowing it was purely intended as a joke. "That's not exactly what I had in mind."

"Not all races appreciate the custom of exchanging gifts," T'Pol reminded him as they reached the launch bay. "Some people may see it as an insult, no matter what the gift."

"Even so, I hate going places empty-handed." Archer tapped a button to open the hatch. "Maybe I'll discuss it with Admiral Forrest during our next briefing."

"If you insist," T'Pol replied as they entered the launch bay.

He had gotten used to T'Pol's tone of disapproving acquiescence; he'd heard it so many times before. *At least I've been hearing it a lot less lately,* he thought as they climbed up to the main level.

"The shuttle's ready for departure, Captain." Lieutenant Malcolm Reed's head popped out the hatch upon hearing their footsteps approaching. "I've completed the preflight."

"Good job, Malcolm," Archer replied, stepping into Shuttlepod One along with Trip and T'Pol. He was always pleased when his ship ran like a well-oiled machine. It was a testament to his own abilities that his hand-picked crew always functioned in top form, especially considering they had departed Earth far earlier than they had planned and, as a result, had been playing catch-up for months. Having the shuttle ready for departure by the time he stepped into the launch bay was what Archer expected of his tactical officer. *Enterprise* was easily becoming *the* example of what a Starfleet ship should be.

Pulling the hatch shut behind them, Reed took his seat at the helm, making final preparations to launch as *Enterprise* hovered in orbit. The planet was a swirling mass of blue and green—somewhat unexpected for a world that was a mining colony.

From the underbelly of the ship, the bay doors slowly opened and Shuttlepod One drop-launched into the cold expanse of space. Reed fired the engines and began the slow and deliberate descent toward the planet. As they approached the atmosphere, sunlight streamed through the pod's ports.

Working judiciously at the helm, Reed was concentrating on the procedures for entering the planet's atmosphere. "This should take a bit longer than usual."

"It wouldn't be very polite to ignite their atmosphere," Archer casually observed, intentionally concealing any tone of concern in his voice. "When are you supposed to close the plasma ducts?"

Focusing on both his captain's question and the task at hand, Reed continued to work the helm. "The protocols said fifty kilometers, but to be on the safe side, I'm going to lock them off at about seventy-five." With a few more buttons Reed confirmed that the plasma ducts were closed and locked. Going over procedures in his head, he double-checked his own work, knowing the importance of the calculations.

As Reed continued working at the helm, Archer knew it was best not to distract the lieutenant, so he busied himself by mentally preparing his opening greeting to the Paraagans. At the same time T'Pol moved up to speak with him on that very same subject.

Taking the jumpseat beside Archer, T'Pol expressed her concern. "Although the matriarchal elements of the culture have diminished, it might be best if I were to ask . . ."

But she never finished the sentence. A series of blinding flashes of light burst through the ports, illuminating the compact shuttlepod, followed by the sounds of a massive explosion.

Archer grabbed for a handhold as the shuttle was rocked hard by a massive shockwave. He watched his crew go flying as the ship was buffeted by the explosion, and he could feel it flipping end over end.

"Report!" he yelled, but knew it was pointless. Reed was no longer attending to the helm, as he had been flung to the side.

The ship tumbled through space and Archer heard a muted thud that he could only assume was one of his crew making hard contact with some part of the ship interior. His senses were assaulted by the sights and sounds of the out-of-control pod as his mind tried to fathom what was going on.

Outside the small vessel a titanic explosion expanded in all directions for kilometers. It began in the heavens as the very air around the shuttle caught fire and spread down to the globe. Flames plumed off the land and spread faster than any wildfire could ever move as the blaze quickly covered the entire world.

Once the blast subsided and the smoke cleared, the swirling blues and greens of the planet were gone—replaced only by scorched and dead land. The ground continued to burn in patches everywhere, looking like small fires from space, but in reality each covered kilometers and kilometers of barren expanse.

Chapter 2

The *Enterprise* bridge crew sat in stunned silence.

They had front-row seats for the holocaust as they witnessed it through the main viewscreen. The explosion seemed to emanate from the shuttlepod and spread through the planet in a matter of seconds, destroying everything in its path. For a moment the entire planet looked like a giant fireball as the shuttlepod was flung through space and off the screen.

Ensign Hoshi Sato ignored the instruments at her station, unable to tear her eyes from the viewscreen. This was exactly the kind of horror the communications officer had imagined in her once frequent nightmares associated with space travel. It had been months since she had let her fears overwhelm her in such a manner, but it was understandable at the moment. *All those people*, she thought. Shaking off the image of herself amid the flames, Hoshi realized there was a job to do.

"*Enterprise* to Shuttlepod One," Hoshi said urgently into the com. "Captain Archer, please respond."

At the helm Mayweather was slightly slower to respond, still stunned by what they had just observed. "Did you see that?"

Hoshi knew that, unlike herself, Ensign Travis Mayweather had spent much of his life in space. He thought of the empty void as home and had probably never witnessed such a horrific event or even imagined it could happen. She could certainly understand his being momentarily frozen as his safe haven turned into a living nightmare.

But Hoshi currently didn't have the time or ability to talk him through it. Instead, she checked her consoles for information on the pod. "The shuttle's attitude isn't right."

"I'm coming around." Mayweather snapped into action, turning the ship as he prepared for the rescue. "Bring the grappler online."

Around them, the rest of the bridge crew started moving as they tore themselves away from the horrible image of the burning planet and took up their roles in the rescue mission. At least, Hoshi hoped it was still a rescue mission and not just one for recovery.

The shuttlepod came back into view as *Enterprise* made the careful turn in its direction. With the burning planet now off the viewscreen, Hoshi could direct her full attention to the pod as it slowly rolled through the scorched atmosphere.

"*Enterprise* to Shuttlepod One," Hoshi tried again. "Come in."

Mayweather glanced at her, silently asking if she heard

anything, but she just shook her head in response. Hitting a few more controls on her console, Hoshi was able to confirm that the grappler was ready.

Mayweather took the grappler controls. "Tell me when," he said to Hoshi.

"We're almost there," she said. Her instruments indicated that the shuttlepod was rolling closer to the ship. The movement would have to be precise. If the grappling arms missed their target, precious time would be wasted retracting them and firing again. Even worse, if they hit the pod at a wrong angle, rather than latching on, the grapplers could ricochet off the vessel, sending it tumbling in another direction and doing even more damage to the already battered team aboard.

Endless seconds passed.

"Hoshi." Mayweather's tension could be felt across the bridge.

"Not yet," she said, never removing her attention from the panel in front of her. "Now!"

Mayweather hit the controls, and the ship fired two grappling devices from beneath the saucer. Slicing through space, the long arms shot out toward Shuttlepod One. Upon contact, the magnetic locking clamps took hold one at a time.

The shuttle stopped its free fall through space. With the clamps locked on, Mayweather slowly reeled the shuttle in, guiding it back toward the ship.

In the limited time Hoshi had spent on *Enterprise* herself, she knew that to consider space to be "dead" was ridiculous. The void surrounding them was teeming with its own form of life, and Mayweather's experience with the cosmos was beneficial to the precise movements he was now required to make. It looked easy enough to just reel the shuttle in, but she knew that looks could be deceiving.

"Bridge to sickbay," Hoshi called into the com, momentarily taking her eyes off the screen.

"Phlox here," came the doctor's response.

"We need a medical team sent to the launch bay."

"On the way."

Hoshi knew the captain would want a report the moment he saw her—if he was even conscious, or alive. She pushed that thought out of her mind, knowing she had a job to do. As Mayweather completed the retrieval of the Shuttlepod One, she turned her full attention to her own instruments, scanning the planet for signs of . . . anything.

It took mere seconds for the information to come up, but what she saw still managed to shock her despite what she'd witnessed on the viewscreen. Refusing to believe the computer, she ran the scans once more, hoping for something positive in the jumble of frightful data. She needed something good to tell the captain—something for the crew to latch on to in what she knew was about to become their most difficult challenge since leaving Earth.

Once more, the information came up on her monitor confirming what she already knew. Hoshi ran the scans again . . . and again.

* * *

Gathered with the senior staff in sickbay, Archer could hear his crew speaking to him, but he was not quite clear on what they were saying. T'Pol and Reed had just gotten off their biobeds, shaken but physically fine. Dr. Phlox was hovering over an unconscious Trip, who had to be carried from the shuttlepod. Archer's worries, however, were not for his friend at the moment. He could only focus on what Hoshi had just reported to him. *How could it be true?* he asked himself. *What have we done?*

"I closed both plasma ducts," Reed insisted, slamming his hand on a biobed in anger and regret. "I'm certain of it."

Archer knew that the lieutenant needed his captain's strength and reassurances, but at the moment he had none to give. Instead, he could only concentrate on Hoshi, hoping that he had heard her wrong. "Are you sure there's nothing left?"

"We could see the colony at full magnification, sir." Her voice was shaky. "The ground is scorched for at least a hundred kilometers in every direction."

"Could one of the dampeners have been malfunctioning?" he asked Reed, hoping for some kind of explanation for the tragic event. He was aware of the fact that there was a slightly accusatory tone in his voice, but he could not help it. *We did this,* he thought.

"I closed both ducts," Reed replied, taking a defensive posture. "Any kind of malfunction would've triggered an alarm—two alarms. There are backups to prevent these kinds of accidents. The ducts were closed!"

And yet, the entire colony has been destroyed. The unspoken words echoed through the captain's mind. He knew that nothing could be done from sickbay, but he wanted as much information as possible immediately, and thus far the crew wasn't providing what he needed.

"This is no time to be placing blame." T'Pol positioned herself between Archer and Reed, trying to break through the heightened emotions of the human crewmembers. "A thorough investigation should explain what happened."

Turning to Phlox, she moved over to the biobed in which Trip was still lying unconscious, attempting to switch the subject to one in which they could have an immediate answer. "How is he?"

"He has a mild concussion, but should be fine," the Denobulan doctor reported while continuing the examination.

But Archer could not be swayed from the topic at hand. "Have you tried hailing the colony?" he pressed Hoshi for more answers. "There has to be *someone* down there."

"Sir, I tried to explain." Hoshi's voice grew firm, not wanting to have to hear herself say the words again. She spoke clearly and concisely. "There's nothing left. No buildings. No trees. No people."

"That's impossible." His shock would not let him believe what she was saying. "There were thirty-six hundred colonists."

Silence hung in the air for seconds, until it was broken by the sound of Trip's belabored breathing. The commander was slowing coming around as the entire senior staff hovered around him.

"Commander Tucker?" Dr. Phlox asked as his patient's eyes flitted open, trying to focus on the bright room and looming shapes surrounding the biobed.

Archer immediately moved to his friend's side.

"Wha-what happened?" he asked groggily.

"We don't know," Archer replied, then added with steel resolve in his voice, "but we're going to find out."

Archer had never before heard the ship so quiet. As he passed through the corridors, nearly every member of his crew was focused on the task of analyzing the information gathered from the Paraagan colony. The relaxed atmosphere he had experienced just a few hours ago was gone. The mood was now that of quiet determination and mournful silence. The captain knew that he should have been arranging some kind of memorial for the lives lost in the cataclysm. *But how do you mourn a colony of people whom you've never met?* he wondered. *How do you ache for lives that you ended?*

He pushed the last thought out of his mind. The facts had not come in yet, and he refused to blame himself for the lives lost. *There will be time to mourn later,* he thought. *Now is the time to act.* But the nagging guilt in his mind was preventing that, and slowly beginning to overpower him. He knew that he needed to be there for his crew, but with with no new information, the job was becoming increasingly difficult.

Departments were sifting through the scans and putting together reports for his review, but no one was working fast enough for him. As Archer stepped into the turbolift, he couldn't help but think that no matter what the reports said, they would never bring back the dead colonists. There was one other undeniable fact: that no matter who or what was the cause of the catastrophe, as the captain of the *Enterprise*, it was he who was ultimately responsible. He tried to push all thoughts from his mind as he rode the lift. The captain prepared himself to receive the answers he had been awaiting.

The turbolift doors opened, and Archer was deposited onto the silent bridge. Each of his senior staff was at his stations, including a now fully conscious Commander Tucker. Moving to T'Pol with quiet desperation, he willed her to have the information he needed. She was the least emotional member of the crew, and he hoped that her straightforward approach to the data would give him the strength he needed.

"Have you finished the diagnostics?" he asked flatly.

"I've analyzed six of the pod's sensor logs," she replied, betraying no emotion over the horror they had apparently caused. "I have two left."

That was not the response he was looking for. "Well, get them done. You've had three hours."

As the science officer continued her work, Archer took the slow walk across the bridge to his friend Trip, knowing that he would have some results.

"What about the *Enterprise* sensor logs?" he pressed. "They must have recorded how much tetrazine there was in the atmosphere. Was the concentration greater than the Paraagans specified? Was it present at higher altitudes than it was supposed to be?"

"That's the weird part, sir," Trip said with a confused expression. "The tetrazine levels were less than three parts per million. That's *half* what the protocols specified."

But Archer didn't want more questions. He wanted answers. "What about the point of ignition?" he asked, turning to Reed. He was running out of crew to satisfy his inquiries.

The lieutenant tapped several buttons at his station to reconfirm the information. "The flash point was directly beneath the shuttle, sir. It seems to have originated at the starboard plasma duct." Reed sounded betrayed by the information he was detailing, but he reported what the computer indicated nonetheless.

"A plasma duct you're certain was closed," Archer said with an edge. His words came out somewhere between question and an acquisition.

"Every log on the shuttle indicates that both ducts were sealed and locked," T'Pol insisted, more to keep the facts straight than out of a need to come to the lieutenant's aide.

"Then you'd better start reexamining those logs." Archer addressed the entire bridge crew, fighting back anger. "Because something doesn't add up here."

Don't screw this up.

Those words had popped into Archer's mind numerous times over the course of their mission, but nowhere near the amount of times they had in the last three hours. It was the last order Forrest had given to Archer on the day he had accepted the challenge to ready *Enterprise* and depart for the Klingon homeworld ten months ago. Archer knew at the time that the admiral had meant the comment only as a lighthearted warning, since both men were well aware of the importance of the mission.

Well, now he *had* screwed up and thirty-six hundred people lost their lives because of it. But even worse was the fact that he had no idea how it had happened. That thought did not sit well with the captain. He knew that his superiors would be even less pleased.

"Get me Admiral Forrest," he said to Hoshi before he added his own lighthearted comment meant to cover the seriousness of the moment, though he was fooling no one. "This is *not* going to be fun."

Chapter 3

"Tetrazine?" Admiral Forrest could scarcely believe what he had just been told—worse, he didn't entirely understand all the aspects of Archer's report. Sitting behind his desk at Starfleet headquarters, it was difficult for him to wrap his head around the fact that thousands had died due to the shuttle's interaction with some substance he had never heard of before.

"It's a by-product of their mining operation," Archer explained in a slow, meticulous manner, seemingly relieved that he could at least account for some part of the events. "It settles between forty-five and fifty kilometers in their atmosphere. Exhaust plasma is about the only thing hot enough to ignite it."

Forrest tried to piece together the puzzle with what little facts Archer had provided. Without the full detailed briefing, it was difficult to do, especially considering he was still in a bit of a shock. "But you said your plasma ducts were closed?"

"Yes, sir," Archer replied. "We're doing everything we can to determine what went wrong, but that's not going to change the fact that there are thirty-six hundred corpses down there."

Forrest could tell that Archer's frustration was quickly giving way to anger, but at the moment he had to focus on the way to properly handle the situation. The interstellar ramifications were too numerous to consider. "Continue to analyze your logs. I'm going to call an emergency meeting of the Command Council." He was not looking forward to this meeting since he already knew how each member of the council would react. "You realize they'll undoubtedly bring the Vulcans into this," he added more for his own benefit than Archer's. "We'll have to figure out who's going to contact the Paraagan homeworld."

"That should be my responsibility, sir," Archer immediately responded. His pain was obvious through the viewscreen. He was wearing a mask of guilt, blame, self-recrimination, and about a dozen other fruitless emotions.

"You're right, it should." It didn't take Forrest's training to realize that he needed to reign the captain in. "But let's take this one step at a time."

"How do you tell all those families that . . ."

"You followed all the protocols that you were given." Forrest could only repeat the information he was provided. This was not the time for questions. That would come later, in numerous meetings and briefings with a variety of people. Now was the time for him to support the captain, so Archer, in turn, could help his crew.

"We came here to meet these people"—Archer's intensity level was on the rise—"to learn something about them. Not to kill them!"

"You followed the protocols!" Forrest insisted, understanding the captain's emotional state but also realizing that a job still needed to be done. "You've got a crew that's going to be looking to you to figure out how to react to all this. Don't let them down." He knew his words were harsh but necessary. "I'll get back to you as soon as I can. I'm sorry, Jon."

One last look at the pained expression on Archer's face and Forrest ended the transmission. He continued to stare at the blank screen, knowing that Archer was doing the same on the other end.

Fifteen minutes ago he had been laughing with a new group of cadets. He was sharing with them some of *Enterprise*'s more thrilling stories of exploration, truly enjoying the looks of wonder and excitement. He knew that each and every one of the cadets dreamed of being assigned to *Enterprise* for its next mission, or possibly one of the ships currently in development. Furthermore, he knew that every active member of Starfleet had that same aspiration. Fifteen minutes ago everything had been so simple and life had been so good.

Of course, that was fifteen minutes ago for the admiral. In that same time he knew the *Enterprise* crew had been checking and double-checking information. And three hours ago, while he was grumbling about his busy schedule, thousands of colonists were dying.

Where do we even start? he thought to himself. Starfleet had prepared for numerous unexpected scenarios inherent in the type of exploration *Enterprise* was conducting, but nothing could ever truly ready them for that type of loss. Somehow, they were going to have to contact a people whom they had never met and explain that an Earth vessel was responsible for the annihilation of an entire colony. *It doesn't help that we don't even know what happened.*

The admiral hit his personal comlink to the outer office. "Lieutenant, get me Commander Williams immediately and alert the rest of the Command Council that we need to meet."

"Yes, sir," his aide responded. "But I believe Ambassador Soval is on his way over from the Vulcan Compound."

Dammit, he thought, *not now.* Taking a breath, he tried to keep emotion out of his voice. "Please contact his people and inform them that I've had to cancel. And Lieutenant, it would be best that this happened *before* he reached headquarters." It was one thing to keep Soval out of the loop for the moment, it was quite another for Forrest to have to lie to the ambassador's face about why he had to cancel the lunch.

"And if they ask the reason for—"

"Make something up!" Forrest was beginning to feel the same anger that he knew Archer was experiencing. He just hoped the captain wasn't taking it out on his crew in the same manner he was with his aide. He balled his fists, hoping to focus all of the stress into his tightly squeezed hands. "And cancel the afternoon schedule."

"Everything?" the lieutenant asked in a hopeless tone.

"Everything!"

"Yes, sir!" His aide snapped to attention at his desk so hard that Forrest practically heard it over the com. The com went dead.

Forrest knew he could rely on his aide to stop Soval before the Vulcan set foot in the building. The kid would then spend the rest of the day clearing the afternoon schedule, and probably have to do the rest of the week as well. For the first time ever, Forrest actually envied the lieutenant. *How I would love for that to be my largest concern for the day.*

Light-years away T'Pol had finished analyzing the pod's sensor logs and found no information that explained the apparent failure of the plasma ducts. The captain had, predictably, not handled the news well; he'd verbally lashed out at her in his ready room. Uncomfortable with his heightened emotional state, T'Pol had excused herself to continue the search for explanations.

"The probe is launched," Mr. Reed reported from his station on the bridge.

"Please keep me advised on your progress," she replied as she stepped into the turbolift. Looking back to the ready room, her feeling of unease around the emotional human crew intensified. As the doors closed, she realized that her own tension level had risen and took a brief moment to enact a meditative exercise to help quell the feeling. She knew that she would have to find time for a more lengthy meditation before the day was out, but for now, that would have to wait.

The turbolift doors opened on D-deck and into a corridor abuzz with activity but she ignored the distraction and continued focusing on the task at hand.

Entering the launch bay, she found Trip with an engineering crew hovering around Shuttlepod One.

"Report," she stated, cutting through any extraneous conversation.

"We've gone over the thing with a fine-tooth comb," Trip said, using one of his customary Earth expressions as he moved to the side of the pod, leaning down by the plasma exhaust ports. "A physical examination of the pod shows that the ducts are closed."

"Could they have been forced shut during the impact from the explosion?" T'Pol asked, knowing the likelihood of such an event was a low.

"That's doubtful," he confirmed. "And it would still bring up the question of why all the sensors read that they were already closed."

"Anything else?" she asked.

"Well, I've been thinking," he said. "If the ports were open, the flash point of the explosion could have ignited the plasma and sent the blast back into the pod. I've been reading the information provided by the Paraagans on tetrazine reactions as well as what we have in the Vulcan database, but the information is limited on that side of the equation."

"A possibility," she concurred. "However, since no one on the ship has experience with these kinds of reactions, it will be difficult to reach a conclusion on your supposition."

"Well, right now all we're gonna have is supposition. This isn't exactly one of them textbook situations!" Trip's emotions boiled up unexpectedly for a moment, and T'Pol was taken aback. "Sorry," he said.

"The captain is depending on us to present him with some facts," she reminded him, ignoring the outburst. "Carry on." T'Pol made her way out of the launch bay.

She continued onto E-deck, gathering information while seeking out solitude. Even finding herself alone in the corridor, she could still feel the mental turmoil of the crew assaulting her senses. It seemed likely to her that the situation would reach a critical point soon, and she would be ill prepared to handle such. In these situations she had learned to rely on the captain's ability to deal with his human crew and provide the stability they required. This time, however, it seemed likely that his behavior was not going to help, and she might have to step in to maintain control. It was not a pleasant concept.

Pushing aside her concerns, she moved onto the one member of the crew that, while quite emotional, did not share in the volatility she had learned to expect from humans.

"Any progress?" she asked as she entered sickbay and found the doctor scrolling through some data on a monitor.

Phlox continued his work as he detailed the few findings thus far. "Mister Reed set the probe down in the center of the colony, but I'm not picking up any biosigns, living or dead. It appears that most everything on the surface was vaporized."

T'Pol found the doctor's concise declaration of the facts to be refreshing. "I've researched the Paraagan's funereal customs," she said, rather matter-of-factly. "It's going to be difficult for them if there are no remains."

His face registered a look of regret that said there was nothing they could do about that. Although it was clear that he would continue the search.

"How's the captain?" Phlox asked what appeared to be an innocent question, though T'Pol suspected otherwise.

"His behavior has been"—she searched for the word—"erratic. He seems to alternate between agitation, despondency, and guilt. He spends most of his time alone. I've tried to remind him that this was an accident, but his responses have been illogical." She paused, reluctant to suggest what she knew to be true. "He seems to be ignoring his responsibilities as captain."

Oddly, Phlox smiled in response. "Ah, to be Vulcan."

T'Pol regarded him with a questioning look.

"It's been my experience that humans have a great deal of difficulty separating emotional despair from what you call responsibility," he explained.

"Nevertheless," T'Pol continued, "as his physician, you should monitor him closely to be certain he remains fit for command."

Phlox's face took on a serious expression. "I understand how"—now he searched for the right word—"uncomfortable his behavior must be for you. But trust me, it would be unnatural for the captain *not* to be affected by grief under these circumstances. It's human nature." His smile returned full strength and larger than any she had seen before. "He'll be fine."

T'Pol did not necessarily agree with the doctor's diagnosis.

Chapter 4

Admiral Forrest and his full staff stepped out of the clamorous conference room. When the door closed behind him, they could still hear the yelling, which seemed rather pointless considering the admiral was no longer there to hear the accusations. As Forrest suspected, the members of the Command Council had taken turns blaming each other for the woes of mankind in their knee-jerk reaction to find fault with someone. He knew from experience that the scapegoat mentality would lessen with time as the council accepted equal responsibility for the decision to start Earth's exploration of the stars. Forrest hoped that they would move to that next stage quickly before Captain Archer was forced to bear the full burden of recrimination.

Luckily, the admiral's staff was well trained to know that they would not speak until he spoke. They had attended the meeting solely as support, ready to run and fetch information as it was needed. His aide took care of them as he silently motioned for each staff member to carry out the jobs that had been detailed for them during the council meeting.

"I am developing one hell of a tension headache," Forrest said to the lieutenant.

"Do you want me to get you something for it?"

"No," he said firmly. "So far it's been the best part of the day."

Once again, Forrest found himself walking down the halls of Starfleet Headquarters. This time, however, his step was much slower, though certainly not lighter. One by one, his staff would break off to numerous sundry destinations until it was just himself and his aide. The kid was blessedly silent as they plodded their way through the halls.

Forrest had briefed the council. The discussions had begun and the planning ensued. Starfleet Headquarters was buzzing with activity. The lieutenant told him earlier that he had already received half a dozen com calls from people outside of Starfleet seeking details on what had happened. In typical fashion bad news had traveled at breakneck speeds, and the admiral knew that it was going to be impossible to keep the *Enterprise* incident from the public for long. But it wasn't the general public who concerned him at the moment.

This is not going to be fun, Forrest thought as they reached the formal receiving room. The chamber was conveniently distant from the main conference room, which Forrest couldn't help but suspect was intentionally done by design.

The door whooshed open and he found Ambassador Soval awaiting his arrival, surrounded by a phalanx of dour-looking Vulcans. *How do people who routinely suppress their emotions always seem to look so miserable?* he thought. *Or maybe that's the reason.*

"Ambassador," he said, trying to maintain a pleasant tone, though he knew even that emotion was not going to be well received. "I'm so sorry I had to cancel our lunch appointment, but a rather pressing situation has come up."

"I see," the ambassador replied in his usual manner, not quite accepting the apology but acknowledging it.

"May we have the room for a moment?" Forrest nodded to his aide, who immediately turned and made his way back out to the corridor. The admiral then waited for a period of time that seemed just short of forever before Soval made his slight nod for his entourage to also vacate the room.

"I trust this pressing situation has something to do with your ill-advised mission into space?"

Forrest focused all his attention on his growing headache, preferring that pain to the discomfort of dealing with Soval. "The matter centers around *Enterprise*," he confirmed.

"They were en route to the Paraagan colony, if I recall correctly." Soval acted as if he was searching his memory for the information, but Forrest had never known the ambassador to be unsure about anything he had said.

"Yes," Forrest confirmed, standing almost at full attention. He had always found this pose to be most relaxing for him when dealing with the Vulcans. It was the one posture that betrayed the least emotion.

"A difficult world to visit," Soval remarked. "Especially if one does not vigilantly navigate the atmosphere."

Forrest suspected the conversation was about to become even more difficult. Once again, he focused his concentration on the growing pain in his head. *He already knows*, the admiral realized. *He knows and he's come prepared with his response.*

MAAGLA FREMAA: OPERATIONS SUPERVISOR
GENDER: FEMALE
AGE: 43
PLACE OF ORIGIN: PARAAGAN SOUTHERN DESERT
TIME ON COLONY: FOUNDING COLONIST

The woman's image held on the monitor in Archer's quarters as he read the brief summary of her life. He hadn't even the chance to meet the operation's supervisor, but he knew her face would haunt him the rest of his days. All of the faces that he was seeing now would be with him forever.

DAAVICO LOANG: EDUCATOR
GENDER: MALE
AGE: 29
PLACE OF ORIGIN: PARAAGAN NORTHERN COAST
TIME ON COLONY: 5 YEARS

He knew that his behavior wasn't productive. He should be on the bridge with his crew, trying to solve the mystery or at least guiding them as they worked on the hopeless task. He knew there were a hundred more things he should be doing as captain and commanding officer, but he could not tear himself away from the screen in his quarters as it showed him more and more images of the Paraagan colonists. Each listing providing only brief clues to a person that no longer existed.

MANDAI BAATL: CHILD
GENDER: FEMALE
AGE: 2 MONTHS
PLACE OF ORIGIN: PARAAGAN COLONY
TIME ON COLONY: 2 MONTHS

With Porthos lying across Archer's lap comfortably unaware of the events of the day, the captain scrolled faster and faster and the images rolled endlessly by his searching eyes. Casually petting the animal with his free hand, Archer found no comfort in the dog's presence.

As images of dozens of colonists continued to scroll by, his thoughts briefly flashed back to the words of Keyla, the mysterious Tandaran woman he had met while vacationing on Risa.

I wouldn't be surprised if they're naming schools after you back on your world.

At the time he thought she was flirting with him, but in reality, the flattery was part of her plan to get him to reveal information on the Suliban. Whatever the motive for her words, they had been pleasant to hear. For Archer to think that children would look up to him in the way he had re-

garded the heroes from his youth—including his own father—was more than he had ever imagined. He had never
been a glory hound and it certainly hadn't been the moti-
vation for his joining Starfleet, but it had been a nice
thought.

Now he would consider himself lucky if future history
would forget Jonathan Archer. But it was far more likely
that the name would instead be long remembered and associated with one of the greatest failures in the archives
of humanity. Or was it possible he would not be remembered as a failure at all, but as a murderer—a man who
had been willing to conquer space at the cost of innocent
lives? It was not farfetched to believe that his legacy could
be seen that way not just on Earth, but throughout the
galaxy as well.

The com chirped, abruptly pulling Archer from his
thoughts. The images on the screen stopped moving as he
tapped the companel. "What is it?"

Hoshi paused on the other end of the comlink, tem-
porarily caught off guard by the anger in Archer's voice.
"It's Admiral Forrest, sir."

An almost immeasurable pause.

"Thank you."

Archer tapped a control, ending contact with the bridge.
Another button and the screen went blank as the thousands of colonists disappeared back into the void. He took
a deep breath before tapping a third control, opening the
transmission with Earth.

* * *

Trip watched as the bridge crew continued scanning every piece of information gathered from the sensors. He knew that, like himself, they were trying not to speculate over the conversation their captain was having with Admiral Forrest. T'Pol, Hoshi, and Mayweather were at each of their stations, while Trip joined Reed at his position.

"The atmospheric analysis from the probe is coming through," Hoshi announced.

"Put it up here, would you?" Reed asked, referring to his monitor.

As Hoshi sent the data to his screen, Trip leaned in so he could also review the data. A look of grim confirmation was apparent on both their faces.

"What is it?" Mayweather asked.

Reed double-checked the data. "The air near the surface is filled with traces of boro-carbons."

The look on the helmsman's face indicated that he did not understand what that piece of information proved.

Trip explained with the help of the research he and Reed had performed earlier, "When tetrazine is ignited by plasma exhaust, there's only one outcome you can be sure of . . ."

"Traces of boro-carbons," Mayweather concluded correctly.

"You got it." Trip was resigned to the fact that their first and only real clue seemed to point in the direction of their guilt.

Reed, however, was not ready to make that jump. "I don't care whether that probe picked up traces of bread pudding. Both our plasma ducts were locked down and there were no leaks in the system. Not unless they miraculously mended themselves afterward."

The captain entered from the turbolift at the end of the outburst. Slowly he crossed the bridge, heading for his ready room. "T'Pol. Trip." He couldn't even bring himself to look at the crew as he asked his senior officers to follow him.

Trip took a moment to shoot a questioning look to his fellow crewmembers as T'Pol walked across the bridge. Together, they entered the ready room and found the captain literally staring into space.

"Sir?" T'Pol asked once the door hissed shut.

Archer couldn't bring himself to say the words.

"Everything okay with Admiral Forrest?" Trip covered his nervousness with questions. "I assume he understands that we . . ."

"We're going home," Archer said in almost a whisper as he turned to face them. "The mission's been canceled."

"Canceled?" Trip couldn't begin to imagine the full meaning of the word.

T'Pol just stood in contemplative silence.

"Our purpose was exploration," Archer said simply.

Trip saw that explanation to be a contradiction. "Exactly!"

"In less than a year," Archer interrupted before his friend could go further, "we've had firefights with over a dozen species. We escalated the conflict between the Vulcans and the Andorians, which included the destruction of one of the Vulcans' most sacred monasteries. We helped eighty-nine Suliban escape from detention. And we just killed thirty-six hundred innocent colonists." To Trip, he sounded more like Ambassador Soval than Captain Jonathan Archer. "Doesn't sound much like *exploration* to me."

"You put it that way, we sound like a band of outlaws," Trip fought on. "But we're not and you know it. We've had to defend ourselves a few times, but we've done nothing to be ashamed of."

Trip's argument fell on deaf ears.

"From what the Admiral tells me," Archer pressed on, numb, "Ambassador Soval will use this to convince Starfleet that we need another ten or twenty years before we try this again."

"Twenty years!" For Trip, things just kept getting worse. "Starfleet won't buy that for a minute."

"Won't they?" Archer asked, trying not to shoot a look at T'Pol. They all knew that she could easily contradict Trip on the persuasive powers of the Vulcan High Command.

Trip, however, turned to T'Pol for support. "Tell him he's crazy! Tell him that's guilt talking, not Jonathan Archer."

T'Pol, however, chose to remain silent.

Knowing she would not respond, Archer addressed her on another, more personal, matter. "A Vulcan ship will meet us in three days to get you and Dr. Phlox." He handed her a padd with the corresponding data. "Please inform Mr. Mayweather to head for these coordinates." He turned back to the port, unable to face them.

Trip's outrage was increasing over the attitude of defeat that permeated the room. "I can't believe you're letting them do this to us! You've waited all your life to command this ship." Then he went in for the kill. "Your father wouldn't have taken this sitting down."

"Dismissed," Archer said softly, staring out the port.

"But, sir—"

"I said you're dismissed." He spun on his friend—his friends. "Both of you."

Trip held the captain's gaze for a tense beat before accepting that the battle was lost. He left the ready room, with T'Pol silently in tow.

As the door shut behind them, Archer turned back to look out to space and the stars; he now believed that his lifelong dream was about to end. *But not just my dream,* he thought. *I've failed my father as well. And that's just the beginning of the list.*

Moments later the stars began to move as *Enterprise* broke orbit of the planet and jumped to warp, heading for home in defeat . . . and disgrace.

Chapter 5

Mayweather made his way through the corridors of E-deck, noticeably dragging a little due to lack of sleep.

"Travis!" a voice called from behind him.

Turning, he saw Crewman Rostov hurrying to catch up with him, and slowed his already lackadaisical pace. "Morning," he said once the crewman had reached him.

"Morning," Rostov said, falling into step with May-weather.

The ensign noticed how neither of them had placed the traditional use of the word *good* before their greeting.

"Any news?" Rostov asked as they continued along E-deck.

"Not that I've heard," he replied. "But I haven't reported for duty yet."

"But if something had happened, they would have called you to duty, right?" the crewman persisted. "I mean if there was some new information."

"Certainly," he replied. "I mean . . . I would imagine so."

"Oh." Rostov couldn't hide his disappointment.

Mayweather stopped outside the mess hall, sensing there was something more on the crewman's mind. "I'm sure if anything of note happens, the captain will make an announcement to the entire crew."

"I know." Rostov didn't sound any more enthused. "It's just . . . how's the captain holding up?"

There were two answers to that question—the truth and the one that would make the crewman more at ease. Mayweather simply decided to go with a third alternate. "I don't know."

"It's weird," Rostov continued. "Ever since we were linked in that alien creature together, I feel closer to the captain, like I understand him better."

Mayweather could certainly understand what the crewman was saying. Rostov had the unfortunate experience of being caught up with Archer, as well Trip, Crewman Kelly, and a security officer, in the body of an alien that had come aboard the ship following their meeting with the Kreetasens a few months back. The weblike creature had trapped them in its tentacles, tapping into their nervous systems and linking their consciousness with itself and with each other. The captives had actually shared each other's thoughts and feelings for a short time while linked.

"At any rate," the crewman continued, "when you talk to the captain, can you let him know I'm behind him? The whole crew is, in fact."

Mayweather was bolstered by the crewman's confidence. He often forgot how little interaction the rest of the crew had with the often busy captain, and had almost taken his own conversations for granted. It felt good to him to be considered a conduit for the crew to speak with their leader. "I will," Mayweather replied. "I'm sure it will be appreciated."

"Thanks," Rostov said as he continued on down the corridor, presumably to share whatever little information he had gleaned from Mayweather with the rest of his friends.

Stepping into the mess hall, Mayweather wasn't really hungry, but knew that he didn't need to add malnutrition to the growing list of problems that had kept him up at night. Looking over the breakfast selections, he couldn't help but suspect that even Chef was feeling the sting of their return home since the morning's choices were rather limited. Without bothering to make a decision, Mayweather loaded his tray with whatever food was nearest him and topped it off with a glass of juice.

Lifting his tray, he went over to join Hoshi, who was already seated at a table. "Sorry I'm late," he said, sitting down with her. "After spending most of the night tossing and turning, I overslept."

"That's okay," she replied. "I can't imagine many people have been having an easy time relaxing since we heard the news."

He looked around the hall and confirmed that everyone else was looking a bit sluggish as well. "I thought Malcolm was joining us."

"He took over from Trip. They have a team in the launch

bay and they've been at it all night," she replied, pushing the food around on her plate. "They must have thirty diagnostic tools down there—three for each member of the team."

Mayweather, too, was pushing the food around, not really in the mood to lift it to his mouth. "I heard Starfleet doesn't want anybody touching Shuttlepod One until they can go over it centimeter by centimeter."

"They're not *touching* anything," she clarified. "Just running analysis after analysis." Mayweather could hear the concern in her voice. "If he doesn't find something soon, Malcolm's going to start believing that he was responsible."

If he doesn't already, Mayweather silently added. He decided to change the subject to something marginally more pleasant. "You think they've replaced you in Brazil yet?"

"Even if they have, they'd take me back," she said wryly. "I'm a prodigy, remember." And they both thought how wasted that talent would be on Earth now. "How about you?"

Mayweather had spent most of the sleepless night weighing his options. "After almost a year on *Enterprise,* the thought of a cargo ship is pretty unappealing."

"What if they made you captain?" She tried to move the conversation in a more positive direction. "You're going to be the most famous boomer around, you know."

"Or maybe infamous." He bristled at the thought. "From what Commander Tucker tells me, the people back home think we're doing nothing out here but getting in trouble."

"Then it's our job to let the 'people back home' know what really happened." She was determined to make the truth be known, even though nothing could be done at the moment. "Anyone who tries to bad-mouth Captain Archer in front of me is going to get an earful . . . in any language they want."

A tense moment passed as they both continued to slide the food around on their plates.

Finally Mayweather broke the silence. "T'Pol's got less than two days left. I never thought I'd say this, but I'm going to miss her."

Hoshi nodded, indicating that she knew what he meant.

More silence ensued.

Mayweather had originally suggested meeting for breakfast as a means of brightening their mood. He had hoped that they could start off the new day with a better outlook. He had been wrong.

Giving up on his meal, Mayweather slid the plate to the middle of the table. "I think I'll get to the bridge."

"Me, too," Hoshi agreed as they both rose and headed for the door.

The day continued in that manner all around the ship. T'Pol had noticed that the anger of the previous day had shifted to melancholy among the entire crew. She had never really seen humans give up so totally on anything before, but as the hours stretched on, the pervading mood became all the more unsettling. Even when the captain made his few appearances on the bridge, the general attitude hardly picked up. In fact, she noticed that his presence appeared to make the crew feel worse, as if they had failed him. Lieutenant Reed seemed to be compensating for his feelings of guilt by overworking the crews in the launch bay.

Nevertheless, when Reed summoned T'Pol to the launch bay long after the day shift had ended, the Vulcan was surprised to find herself hurrying. Reed had not told her what was so urgent that it required her presence, and her systematic mind refrained from making guesses, but somehow getting to the launch bay quickly seemed . . . logical.

She saw Reed with a half dozen rather fatigued crewmembers all hunched over various diagnostic tools scanning the pod. She was tempted to point out that they had been ordered to leave the shuttle alone, but the lieutenant was obviously aware of the fact, so she simply made her presence known.

"Lieutenant?" she said when he failed to look up upon her arrival.

"Over here," he said, studying a portable monitor, and not bothering to make eye contact. He turned the monitor in her direction, indicating a collection of data. "It's not exactly a smoking gun, but this EM signature doesn't belong here."

T'Pol ignored the curious "smoking gun" comment as she looked over his information. "Where did you find it?"

"On the outer hull," he replied. "About twelve centimeters behind the starboard plasma duct."

"It might simply be boro-carbons formed by the explosion," she suggested, not wanting to rule out any possibilities. Reed's manner had been growing increasingly erratic since the accident. She didn't want to give him false hope in case he responded with an overly emotional response.

"I already checked." His body tensed. "There isn't a carbon atom to be found. Whatever it is, its profile doesn't match anything in our database."

T'Pol considered the data for a moment. Like everything else, it had only raised more questions, rather than presenting definitive answers. Still, it might be a valid discovery. "I'll take it to the captain," she replied. "In the meantime, I think it would be best if you let the team go and you got some rest yourself."

"I'm fine," he insisted.

"You have not been to bed since the accident," she reminded him. "If this investigation is to continue, we are going to need the entire crew at their most alert."

He remained silent.

"I could make it an order, Lieutenant," she reminded him.

Reed gave her a look of resignation that confirmed he knew she was right. Turning to his team, he said, "That's enough for today. Let's wrap this up . . . for now."

In his quarters Archer banged a water polo ball against his bent knee. A match played on the monitor beside him, but he was not watching it, as he was lost in the *would'ves* and *could'ves* going through his mind. Out of his uniform and dressed in his civvies, he knew that sleep was still hours off, although Porthos seemed to be trying to get some rest curled up on his pillow on the floor.

The door chimed.

"Come in," he called out, without getting off the bed.

T'Pol entered, carrying a padd with the information she had collected in the launch bay.

"What was so important it couldn't wait till morning?" he bluntly asked.

"If you'd prefer, I'll come back," she replied, turning back to the door.

"No, I'm sorry." He hit a button to stop the playback of the game and sat up. "What have you got?" He couldn't quite bring himself to sound interested, but he wasn't going to be entirely dismissive.

She handed him the padd, explaining what Reed and his team had found on the hull of the shuttlepod.

Archer stared at the data, surprised by the fact that T'Pol seemed to be grasping at straws. "It could be anything." He tossed her the ball.

"Mister Reed felt you'd be interested," she insisted, tossing it back.

"In what?" His frustration came out once again. "Does he think that Starfleet Command is going to take a look at this, apologize, and send us on our way?" He realized that he had crossed the line. He handed the padd back to her and went to get Porthos his dinner. "Tell him it was a nice try."

T'Pol, however, didn't leave. "Is this what humans refer to as 'feeling sorry for themselves'?" she asked, as much in honest curiosity as to make a point.

"You're out of line, Sub-Commander."

"I apologize," she said, though not entirely meaning it.

She turned to leave, assuming that the conversation had ended.

"I wish I was simply feeling sorry for myself." He stopped her as he put the bowl in front of Porthos. "But actually, I'm feeling sorry for a whole lot of people—every member of Starfleet, in fact. Their futures depended upon my ability to succeed at this mission." He threw himself back into his bed.

T'Pol proceeded carefully, knowing the full weight of what she was about to say. "As soon as we learned about the consequences of the explosion, I knew the Vulcan High Command would take advantage of the situation."

"What's your point?" he asked, focusing on the obviousness of her comment but admiring the fact that she actually had the Vulcan equivalent of the courage to say it.

"You have a responsibility to dispute their recommendation."

"Starfleet already bought their recommendation hook, line, and sinker."

"Then you have a responsibility to convince *them* as well," she insisted.

"And just how do you suggest I do that?"

T'Pol paused for a moment to prepare her argument. "You were very adept at listing the questionable decisions you've made," she reminded him of their earlier conversation. "But there have been other decisions—many of them—that no one would question. I'm willing to try to convince *my* government of that. Are you willing to try to convince *yours?*"

The question hung in the air.

Archer was pleasantly surprised by her offer and finally softened with even a bit of a smile forming. "You know, this has got to be the first time a Vulcan has ever attempted to cheer up a human."

T'Pol chose to leave his comment hanging. "I'll see you in the morning."

On another part of E-deck, there was more unusual activity at the increasingly late hour. Having finished his shift a few hours before and willing to sleep, Trip needed something to do.

First he had sought out T'Pol hoping to spend some time with her before she left the ship. The two had been moving toward a friendship, so he wasn't surprised to find that he was sad that the Vulcan was about to be out of his life, probably for good. He knew that she certainly wouldn't have expressed the same feelings of camaraderie, but it would have been nice to spend a little more time with her. Unfortunately, Mayweather told him that she had been called away by Lieutenant Reed before the commander could find her.

Failing that, Trip decided to visit with Phlox for a bit. He felt as if he had hardly gotten to know the doctor, and now he too would be gone. It was only one of the regrets over things he hadn't managed to do during their mission.

"Commander, could you hand me that diagnostic tool?" Phlox asked, indicating a table beside one of the biobeds in sickbay.

"This one?" he asked, holding up one tool from a collection neatly lain out on the table. When he had entered sickbay he found the doctor, rather cheerily packing up his things, and offered to help.

"No, no, that belongs to Starfleet." Phlox smiled. "I'm only taking what I brought aboard."

Trip put the tool back down. "I'd take whatever you want. This ship is most likely gonna end up in mothballs in a couple of weeks." He moved over to a small group of cages, curious as to their contents. As he reached for one, a strange alien chirping began, that quickly became quite agitated, causing him to jump back. *At least somebody here other than me is not happy,* he thought.

"That's all right, Commander." Phlox came over to the cage to put the critter at ease, carefully guiding Trip away. "Your company is appreciated, but it would be best if you left the packing to me."

"I would've thought you'd be a little more upset about leaving *Enterprise,*" Trip commented as the doctor continued to pack.

"I did expect this posting to last a while longer, but I'm sure an equally adventurous opportunity will present itself."

"I wish I had your attitude," Trip said, although he couldn't imagine ever just thinking of this mission as a simple *posting.*

"Humans seems to be naturally optimistic," Phlox noted with a smile. "I'm surprised you don't share my outlook that something exciting is always waiting around the next nebula."

Trip was amazed by the fact that Phlox seemed to be ignoring the obvious. "That's just the point," he reminded the doctor. "There won't be any nebulas in Starfleet's future. At least not for a decade or so."

"Oh, I wouldn't be so sure of that," Phlox said with his cryptic brand of optimism.

"You're wrong, Doc." Trip's anger was building, much as it had been since they found out the mission was canceled and they had been recalled. "You worked with Vulcans. You know what they think of us." Trip needed to move. He needed to do something. "*Enterprise* coming back to Earth with its tail tucked between its legs. It'll be Soval's crowning achievement. They'll probably give the son of a bitch some gaudy medal and then cart him off to wherever they send bitter old Vulcans to retire!"

"Ambassador Soval's service record contains an impressive list of accomplishments," the doctor noted as he went on with his packing.

"You have to find something good in everybody, don't you?" Trip knew that to be an admirable quality, but in the current moment of frustration, praise for the bitter old Vulcan was the last thing he wanted to hear. "I gotta tell you, that's one of your *unique qualities* that drive me crazy!"

Despite Trip's outburst, the doctor cheerfully continued to do what he was doing with a bit of a chuckle. "I'll certainly miss your outspoken personality, Mister Tucker."

How do you argue with someone who won't argue back? Trip wondered. With an exasperated sigh of resignation, he realized that his little visit was not the calming conversation he had been searching for. "I'll see you later, Doc."

Trip headed for the door, lost in his thoughts. As it

opened, he nearly barreled right into Crewman Elizabeth Cutler.

"Oh, hi, Commander," she said, stepping out of the way.

He did little more than grunt in response.

The door shut behind him.

"I see the commander's in pretty much the same mood as the rest of the crew," she said to Phlox, who appeared to be absorbed in categorizing medications.

"I would say so," he absentmindedly responded, separating the medicines into containers for himself and Starfleet. "Is there something I can do for you?"

Cutler smiled. "I think that's what I'm supposed to be asking you."

Phlox was momentarily confused by her comment.

"I'm here to help pack," she said, "remember?"

"Oh, that's right, I forgot," Phlox said as he put the last bottle in the Starfleet container. "Everyone does want to be so helpful all of the sudden."

"I think we're all just looking for something to keep our minds off things," she said, sitting up on a biobed. Her feet swung casually.

"It was a tragedy," Phlox agreed.

"Yes, it was," she said. "And it just keeps getting worse."

"Now, now." Phlox remained positive. "I don't need to go over the same things I've said to Mr. Tucker. I'm sure Starfleet will have some plan for the future of this program."

"I was actually referring to you leaving the ship," she said. "I feel like we were just starting to really get to know each other. I'm going to miss you."

The doctor was a little taken aback. Their friendship had always confused him a little. She was so unlike Denobulan women, especially his wives. "Well, yes," he replied uncomfortably. "I'll miss you as well. Along with the rest of the crew."

"Of course," she said with a playful grin at his suddenly formal tone, "you've been an invaluable resource."

"I do hope you have a chance to keep up with your studies," he replied in reference to the medical tutoring he had been providing her.

"Oh, yes," she said, having some fun. "And I hope you have a chance to keep up with your three wives."

Now the doctor was actually flustered. He wasn't sure if they were flirting or if she was being serious. *Maybe I should have spent some more time studying human behavior while I had the chance.*

"At any rate," she said, hopping down from the bed, "I will miss you as more than just a valuable resource." Leaning in she gave him a slightly prolonged kiss on the cheek.

For about the hundredth time since Phlox had met Elizabeth Cutler, she had rendered him speechless.

"Well," she said with a giggle, "we should really finish up this packing. It's getting late."

Chapter 6

"Come on, Porthos," Archer said, rubbing behind his beloved pet's ear. "Time for bed."

He had stripped down to his blue shorts and tank and lain back on his bed, ready to let another day mercifully end. Archer knew that sleep probably would not come—as it hadn't the night before. Mulling over his regrets in the dark wasn't much different than considering them in his waking hours. Preparing himself for the long night of remorse, he turned off the lights.

He patted on the bed beside him. "Porthos, up!"

In the brief moments of silence that followed, his subconscious mind picked up on the subtle changes. The sheets felt different against his chest. In fact, they now covered him, rather than lying beneath him. The bed felt different. Even the air smelled different—familiar, but different—certainly not the recycled atmosphere he had been breathing for the past several months.

And yet, his conscious mind had not quite grasped the significance of the changes. He had notice that Porthos still wasn't beside him. "What's the matter, boy?" he reached for the light. "Don't tell me you're . . ."

The lights came back on, leaving Archer shocked by his surroundings. He was back in his apartment in San Francisco. Leaning up on an elbow, he noticed that the place looked exactly as it had before he had closed it up and left on his mission.

Pushing the covers back, Archer found himself now dressed only in pajama bottoms. Understandably disoriented, he moved to the window, pulling back the sheer white curtains to confirm that the San Francisco skyline was indeed outside.

"Porthos." He bent to find his pet curled up in a doggy bed, also awake. "What's going on here?" He didn't expect the dog to answer, but considering that he had just traveled thousands of light-years in the blink of an eye, it wouldn't be the largest surprise if Porthos had suddenly gained the power of speech.

The chirp of a companel pulled Archer away from his pet. Stepping down into the sunken living room of his studio apartment, Archer tapped the wall panel, wondering who could be calling and if that person had any answers.

"Hello?" he tentatively greeted the caller.

"Sorry to call so late, Captain," the voice of his friend, Trip, came over the com system. "But all three inspection pods are getting their weekly overhauls tonight. They tell me they won't be ready until noon. So I figured you might . . ."

". . . want to sleep in," he whispered in concert with Trip as he finished the statement. Archer hesitated, realizing that he had gotten this call before. It had been shortly before his life had taken a major turn.

"What do you say to breakfast at nine-thirty," Archer suggested, testing the waters with his recollection of events. "Spacedock cafeteria?"

"You must be reading my mind," Trip confirmed with a smile that could be heard over the com. "I was just about to suggest the same thing."

Archer wanted to talk to his friend about what was going on, but since Trip didn't seem to notice anything out of place, the captain decided against it. "See you in the morning."

He tapped a control, shutting off the com, his mind grappling with all the possible explanations. "If you're trying to tell me the last ten months was a dream," he said to Porthos, the only other body in the room, "I'm not buying it."

Considering his options, Archer came up with an idea to test his unlikely theory. Moving into the main living area, he bent over his desk, tapping another companel, which activated a monitor screen. Scrolling through a series of data, he found the information he was looking for and hit the appropriate commands.

After a beat a receptionist popped up on the screen. She looked quite awake, considering the late hour.

"I.M.E. Can I help you?" she asked, looking back through her own monitor.

"This is Jonathan Archer." His mind was still focused on his predicament. "Starfleet authorization Alpha-Six-Four—"

"I know who you are, Captain," she interrupted him. "What can I do for you?"

Ah, the price of fame, he mused, wondering how soon it would be before people started recognizing him for less pleasant reasons. But he had more pressing matters at the moment. "Do you have a Denobulan doctor in the Interspecies Medical Exchange?"

The woman referenced his question on a nearby screen. "Yes, a Doctor Phlox." She continued to scroll through the information in front of her. "He's assigned to Starfleet Medical here in San Francisco. Would you like me to contact him for you?"

"No, that's all right," Archer replied, not knowing what he would say if he had managed to speak with the doctor. Besides, he had gotten the information he needed. "Thanks for your help."

He tapped another button and the screen blinked off. Turning back to Porthos, he continued to go over the little clues he had been collecting since the lights came on. "I didn't even know Phlox existed before they brought Klaang in. And that was the day *after* I got the late-night call from Trip."

"You're not dreaming, Captain," a familiar voice said from behind him.

Archer whirled to see a man who should have been

dead. He was stepping out of the shadows, dressed in a Starfleet uniform—looking exactly as Archer had seen him before his supposed demise.

"Daniels."

"This must be very disorienting," Daniels said, looking contrite. He was wearing his Starfleet uniform, though Archer knew that the man was not a part of the organization. "I apologize, but I had no choice."

Still suspicious, Archer moved past the apology in search of information. "Commander Tucker told me you were dead. That Silik killed you."

"He did," Daniels cryptically replied. "In a manner of speaking." But Daniels did not intend to get into an explanation on his miraculous recovery from death. "We have to talk, Captain, and it's essential that none of the other factions know about it. I doubt any of them would think I'd bring you here."

By *here*, Archer knew that he wasn't talking about San Francisco. "So you're telling me you brought me back . . . what . . . ten months ago?" He could not believe what he was saying. "How about Jonathan Archer ten months ago? Where's he?"

"He's you."

"Then who just climbed into bed aboard *Enterprise?*"

"That hasn't happened yet."

And is Porthos really Porthos or did he come back in time, too? Archer thought. Instead he said, "That's a load of crap and you know it."

Daniels had a look of annoyed frustration on his face as

64

he took a seat. "I've had this conversation with half a dozen people. It always turns out the same way."

Well, you've never had it with me, Archer thought, offended by the dismissive attitude he was receiving. "Can't you ever give a straight answer?"

"It depends on the question."

Archer knew that he had to choose his words carefully until he figured out what kind of game Daniels was playing. "All right, try this one. Why am I here? I thought you were supposed to protect the timeline, not screw with it."

"It's already been 'screwed with,' Captain," he said, choosing to use Archer's own colorful language to explain. "That explosion at the Paraagan colony . . . it wasn't supposed to happen."

"Of course it wasn't," Archer replied. "It was an accident."

"That's not what I mean," Daniels tried to explain. "History never recorded the disaster. Someone violated the Temporal Accord . . . someone who doesn't want your mission to succeed."

How is our mission dangerous? We're simply exploring, Archer thought. He sat down as his mind latched on to a more important concept. "Are you telling me that *Enterprise* didn't cause that explosion?"

Daniels eyed him, choosing not to answer the question. "Do you remember the Temporal Cold War I spoke of?"

"It's kind of hard to forget," Archer replied, still awaiting a straightforward answer.

"Then listen to me carefully," Daniels insisted. "We don't have much time."

Archer did listen carefully as Daniels detailed the plan. What the man was saying seemed impossible, and yet, Archer was sitting in the middle of his living room, which he knew to be an equally infeasible feat. Slowly the pieces began to fit together. Archer realized how coincidental it was that these events seemed to be set in motion the moment he had stepped into the captain's mess with Trip and T'Pol both one day ago and ten months from now. That was the room on *Enterprise* where he had come to know this time traveler who was standing before him. Of course back then he had thought Daniels to be nothing more than a simple steward.

Chapter 7

September 2151
Six Months Ago

Archer sat alone at the table of his private mess, reading a padd and sipping a cup of coffee, preparing himself for the day ahead. One of his stewards, Crewman Daniels, entered carrying a plate of scrambled eggs.

"Good morning, sir," the steward said as he set the eggs down in front of the captain.

"Morning, Daniels," he replied. "I thought this was Taylor's shift."

"I switched with him," Daniels tentatively replied, "if that's all right with you."

"No problem."

"Sir, I noticed we changed course. May I ask why?"

"There's a stellar nursery not far from here," Archer replied with a sip of his coffee. "We detected several ships inside and thought we might go say hello."

"Very good, sir." Daniels seemed to consider the captain's words for a moment. "More orange juice?"

"I'm fine, thanks," Archer replied as he watched Daniels nod and head out of the room.

Archer leisurely concluded his breakfast and made his way to the bridge, where the crew eventually made contact with one of the vessels in the stellar nursery. It was a transport vessel led by a somewhat dour captain named Fraddock. After an initially terse greeting, Fraddock eventually warmed to Archer, informing him that the transport vessel was carrying a group of "spiritually minded" passengers on a pilgrimage to the Great Plume of Agosoria.

Fraddock described the stellar phenomena, and it sounded intriguing enough for Archer to welcome the transport captain and the pilgrims to visit *Enterprise* as the Starfleet crew joined them on their journey. Fraddock gruffly declined, but the passengers welcomed the opportunity. The two vessels docked together shortly thereafter as Captain Archer received his guests and unknowingly allowed a Suliban to come aboard.

Following a celebratory meal, one of the pilgrims asked about a tour of *Enterprise*. The hospitable captain split the group in two, placing Trip in charge of several of their guests as an escort through the ship while he took the rest of the pilgrims around. In engineering, Trip led his group through the inner workings of the warp core, as one of the pilgrims slipped away from the group unnoticed.

The rogue pilgrim ducked behind the warp core. Eyeing an access port above him, he opened the panel and reached an arm into the jumble of circuitry. His arm continued reaching deeper into the cramped panel, twisting at an impossible angle to allow for his hand to reach a particular metal conduit. Once it was in his grasp, the pilgrim twisted the conduit out of shape, disconnecting it from an adjoining piece. His job done, he replaced the panel and joined his group, never having been missed.

"You might want to focus your sensors on that plasma storm up ahead," Fraddock cockily announced via the main viewscreen while Archer and Trip were busy with the tours.

"We're aware of it," T'Pol replied.

"You ever been in a plasma storm?"

"Twice."

"Then you know it can get a little bumpy," Fraddock said, obviously disappointed that his new acquaintances were familiar with the occurrence. "I suggest we try to go around it."

"Agreed." She nodded to Mayweather. "Ensign?"

"I'm already on it," he replied, working the helm.

Though they managed to circumnavigate the brunt of the storm, the outer edge of it still wrecked havoc on the ship, forcing the captain to abandon his tour group. The ship jolted through the storm as tendrils of plasma lighting lashed out at the vessel. Lights were flickering on the bridge as the captain came off the turbolift.

"Report," he called over the noises on the bridge.

"We're losing main power," Reed said, consulting his station.

Reaching a companel, Archer called down to engineering. "Trip, what's happening?"

"That last bolt struck the warp manifold! We've got an antimatter cascade, sir!" Trip answered back, working frantically at a station by the warp reactor. The power was rising and falling erratically as all but one of the pilgrims looked on with concern. "If it reaches the reactor we're gonna—"

BOOM!

A panel blew out in a shower of sparks as everyone in engineering took cover.

B-BOOM-BOOM-BOOM!

Several more panels and consoles exploded in quick succession, heading for the warp reactor. One by one the explosions continued, until they reached the panel beside the one on which the stowaway pilgrim had been working. Then the blasts suddenly stopped, with an electrical crackling sound coming from the last panel, but nothing more. In the resulting silence, everyone in engineering took a deep breath as Trip checked a nearby readout.

Switching on the nearest companel, he reported to the bridge. "I think we're all right, Captain. The cascade stopped in its tracks."

"Good work, Trip," Archer answered back.

"It wasn't me, sir."

It didn't take Trip long to discover the antimatter junction that was disconnected and realize they had a guardian angel onboard looking after the crew. The only problem was they didn't know that their angel was in the form of an old enemy.

Walking down a corridor mulling over Trip's discovery, Archer was approached by Crewman Daniels.

"Sir, I need to speak with you," the crewman said urgently.

"Why don't you talk to one of my bridge officers," Archer suggested, distracted by his thoughts. "I'm a little busy right now."

"It's important."

"I'm sorry, Daniels," he replied, still moving. "I've got my hands full."

"It's about the Suliban."

This stopped Archer in his tracks.

"What about them?" he asked, his interest piqued. What information could his steward possess about an enemy they had not had contact with in four months?

"I have reason to believe that one of the pilgrims who came aboard is a Suliban soldier." He paused waiting for the captain to ingest what he was saying. "His name is Silik. He's the man you fought with on the Helix."

"How the hell did you know what I did on the Helix?" he asked, in reference to the space station comprised of hundreds of Suliban cell-ships.

Daniels glanced at a nearby crewmember passing by in an adjacent corridor. "It might be best if we discuss this in private," he said in a low voice.

"My ready room," the captain replied.

"I think it would be better if we went to my quarters," Daniels suggested instead.

"Why?"

"You'll understand when we get there, sir," Daniels cryptically replied.

Archer hesitated for a moment wondering what the hell

was going on. In only a few words Daniels managed to reveal that he knew far more than anyone in his position on *Enterprise* should have known. *This is more than just random gossip being spread*, Archer thought. He nodded to Daniels, indicating that he would follow.

Once they reached the cramped quarters, Daniels showed the captain inside. "Please have a seat."

But Archer preferred to stand.

"I'm sorry about the mess." Daniels indicated the items strewn about as he reached inside his locker. "Sometimes I think my bunkmate majored in chaos theory."

But Archer was not in the mood for humor, either. He wanted answers and he wanted them now.

Daniels pulled a small equipment case from the locker. Opening it, he removed a hand-held device that looked to Archer like no piece of technology he had ever seen before.

"What is that?" Archer asked. "That doesn't look like Starfleet issue."

"That's because I'm not a member of Starfleet," Daniels simply stated. "Not that I wouldn't be honored to be one, sir, especially after spending time—"

"Who are you?" Archer interrupted, getting right to the point. The man had somehow infiltrated his crew for four months. This was not just some simple stowaway. "How do you know what happened on the Helix?"

"Did Silik tell you who he was working for?" Daniels asked instead.

"I'm the one asking questions, Crewman."

Daniels calmly pressed on. "Did he mention the Temporal Cold War?"

"What do you know about that?" Archer continued to be surprised by the wealth of information Daniels seemed to possess.

"A great deal more than you do, sir," was his simple reply.

Archer was growing impatient with the non-answers. "If you're not a member of Starfleet, then who are you?"

"I work for a different kind of organization," he replied, still intentionally vague. "We make sure that people like Silik don't interfere with historical events."

"I've never heard of a group like that," Archer replied, wondering what kind of "historical events" the man was referring to.

"That's because it doesn't exist yet."

Archer eyed the crewman curiously. "So you're telling me you're some kind of time traveler?"

"That's one way of putting it." Daniels indicated the device he had taken out. "Maybe this will help clear things up."

Daniels hit a few controls on the instrument, and the entire room shimmered around them. It was replaced by a three-dimensional graphic display of timelines, planets, alphanumeric data, strange symbols, mathematical equations, and hundreds of other graphics that Archer could not discern. Everything was scrolling around them and flying past. It was a mind-boggling display of information.

Daniels did not seem even the least bit phased by it. "This is how we keep an eye on what's going on. You might call it a 'Temporal Observatory.'"

Archer was glancing around, trying to wrap his mind around what he was seeing.

Daniels saw the confusion on the man's face. "I know this must seem a little overwhelming. . . ."

"*Overwhelming* doesn't quite cover it." Archer reached out to touch one of the images floating in front of him, surprised that the projection of light actually had weight to it.

"I come from right about here," Daniels said, pointing to a timeline graphic. "Approximately nine hundred years from now."

"Are you human?" Archer asked, remembering that the Suliban had the ability to alter their appearances.

"More or less," he said with another cryptic response.

"And the people giving Silik orders?"

"They're from an earlier century. From about here." He indicated another coordinate back on the timeline. "They can't manifest themselves physically in the past. They can only partially materialize to deliver information."

"But not you."

"In the years that followed," Daniels explained, "we eventually perfected the process."

"Sounds dangerous," Archer commented, giving up on questions for the moment since he knew most of them would continue to go unanswered.

"When time travel first developed, it wasn't long before people realized that laws had to be made," he explained. "All the species who had the technology agreed that it would only be used for research."

"But it wasn't," Archer said, catching on. "That's what the Temporal Cold War is all about."

Daniels nodded and explained that Silik had been the one to prevent the reactor breach and save the ship. Daniels had been sent back in time to capture the Suliban soldier but he would need the crew's help tying his technology into the *Enterprise* sensor grid to track the genetically modified alien.

"We have reason to believe that the twenty-second century is a front in this Cold War," Daniels went on. "What happens here could affect millennia to come. It's imperative that we find out who Silik is working for and what they're trying to do."

There was much to consider, and Archer consulted with the most reliable members of his staff, Trip and T'Pol. He wanted their opinions as to whether he could trust a man who had been lying to them for months, and whether or not they felt that the being who'd saved their ship from destruction was actually an enemy.

Although Trip kept an open mind, T'Pol's response was typical of her people's almost innate cynicism. "The Vulcan Science Directorate has studied the question of time travel in great detail. They've found no evidence that it exists or that it can exist."

Still, no matter what their personal feelings, both officers went along with Archer's decision to help "Crewman Daniels" set up the sensor grid. Along the way, they hit a bit of a snag.

"One of the power relays is offline," T'Pol said as the trio worked in engineering.

"Must've been damaged in the plasma storm," Trip guessed as he checked a monitor. "J-thirty-seven. It's about three meters behind that bulkhead." He pointed to a nearby wall.

"I'll take care of it," Daniels said. He pulled a tiny device from his equipment case and placed it over the fingers of his right hand. "J-thirty-seven?"

Trip nodded, wondering what the so-called future visitor was up to. He watched in astonishment as Daniels activated the device and casually walked right through the bulkhead. Trip looked to T'Pol, who took in the strange sight with very little apparent reaction whatsoever.

Moments later Daniels came back out through the wall. "Try it now."

Trusting the three to work in engineering without him, Archer retired to his quarters. He had been so busy that morning that he not only forgot to feed himself, but had left Porthos wanting as well. However, as hungry as the dog was, he seemed also preoccupied with something in the room. Porthos was barking at something or someone. Archer realized he was not alone and reached for his companel.

"If you're thinking of calling for help, I'd advise against it." Silik became visible as he phased out of his camouflage into the familiar Suliban flesh and clothing Archer had seen him in months ago. "I'm not the one you should be worried about, Jon."

"What are you doing here?" Archer asked guardedly.

"I thought you might want to thank me."

Archer chose not to respond.

"I saved your life," Silik announced, confirming what Daniels had claimed. "The least you could do is return the favor. There's someone here trying to find me. I need to know who it is."

"I don't know what you're talking about," Archer said. It wasn't entirely a lie.

"I detected tachyon radiation," Silik explained. The terminology was unfamiliar to Archer so he didn't respond. "You don't have anything that emits tachyons," Silik continued, his expression grew intense. "Who's looking for me?"

"I don't know," Archer replied evenly.

The two continued their dance around the truth, with Silik suggesting that the group he was working against actually wanted *Enterprise* destroyed. He claimed that it was the *other* group that was interested in tampering with the timeline. But Archer had reason to distrust Silik and refused to give Daniels up. Ultimately, however, the two were interrupted by a call from T'Pol that gave Silik the answer he was looking for. Silik fired his weapon at Archer, rendering the captain unconscious before heading for engineering to find Daniels.

Meanwhile, in engineering, Daniels, Trip, and T'Pol had successfully prepared the sensor grid and were able to pick up Silik's camouflaged presence on the ship, nearing their position. Although the technology did not allow them to pinpoint the Suliban's exact location, an unexplained sound above them told them everything they needed to know.

"You two should go," Daniels said, tense.

"We're not leaving," Trip replied.

"Go!" he insisted. "Bring help!"

Trip and T'Pol reluctantly moved toward the hatch in search of Reed and the security team they had called for. But before they could leave, Silik materialized and dropped from a catwalk above. Daniels spun to find a pistol leveled at him.

"Did they tell you that the twenty-second century was going to be your final resting place?" Silik fired his weapon.

Daniels stumbled backward as his body shimmered and distorted. He tried to reach for his pistol, but Silik fired again. This time the contact was far more devastating, and Daniels's entire body shattered into fragments, evaporating as he flew apart.

Trip looked at T'Pol in shock, but when they looked back at Silik, the Suliban was gone.

Trip reported the incident to the captain, once Archer regained consciousness. After determining the camouflaged Silik was still on the ship, every outer-door and exit hatch was locked and security teams were posted on each deck.

Hurrying to Daniels's quarters, Archer had a feeling of doom that was justified when he opened the small equipment scanner he had been shown earlier. The space-time scanner that Daniels had used to create his "Temporal Observatory" was gone. Silik had it. *He's not going to get off my ship with that technology,* Archer promised himself.

Trip had difficulty interpreting the futuristic sensors in search of the Suliban, but the technology proved unnecessary when the *Enterprise* computer alerted them to the fact that someone was trying to bypass the lock-out codes for Launch Bay Two. As Archer headed for Silik's position, Trip gave the captain something that might help against the genetically advanced alien.

Archer met up with Reed and his security team in a corridor beside the junction in which Silik was working.

"It looks like he slipped through here," Reed said, regarding the panel. "We could remove these conduits, but it would take some time."

Archer eyed the panel, then considered the device that Trip had given him. It was resting in his right hand. He tapped a control on the device.

"Sir?" Reed said as Archer tentatively reached his hand out toward the circuitry and passed right through it.

"Stay here." Archer took a deep breath and, steeling himself for the bizarre experience, carefully walked to the bulkhead and phased through.

Passing through metal and wiring, Archer found himself in a cramped, dimly lit passageway filled with crisscrossing conduits, exposed circuitry, and Silik. The Suliban soldier was standing at a small hatch on the wall, reworking some circuits.

"Very clever." Silik turned to find Archer's weapon raised. "Careful, Jon," he said, motioning toward the circuitry. "It'd be a shame if you triggered another antimatter cascade. There'd be nobody here to stop it."

"Put that device on the floor," he said, referring to the space-time scanner.

"It would be in your best interest to let me take it," Silik replied simply.

Archer didn't believe the Suliban. "You keep saying you're here to help us. But I can't help wondering what kind of genetic enhancements you'll get for bringing back that little prize. Eyes in the back of your head? A pair of wings?"

Silik's expression darkened. "That's a cynical attitude, Jon. I thought your species was more trusting."

The ship trembled from the protostar reactions as the Great Plume of Agosoria flared with a burst of energy. As the reactions grew they caused the ship to bounce violently about, knocking both men off balance. Silik seized upon the opportunity and rushed Archer.

The pair struggled against each other, both losing their weapons. Gaining the upper hand, Silik buffeted Archer's body with savage blows, knocking the captain to the deck, dazed. Moving back to the panel, Silik managed to open the hatch and climbed into the launch bay precisely at the moment the bridge crew discovered a Suliban vessel approaching.

Moving to the launch bay control panel, Silik found the instrument necessary to open the bay doors.

"I'm not going to ask you again," Archer said from behind the alien, holding his phase pistol. "Put it down."

"You're going to kill me after I saved your life?" Silik replied.

A tense moment followed as Archer stared down the

Suliban. Lowering his aim, the captain fired, striking the space-time scanner and blowing it out of Silik's hand. The device skittered across the deck, charred and destroyed.

"You may have endangered your future, Jon," Silik said angrily and then dashed out into the launch bay, camouflaging himself once again.

As Archer followed, a Klaxon sounded, signifying that the hydraulics had engaged. Knowing what that meant, Archer grabbed hold of a nearby railing on a catwalk just in time as the bay doors opened and the entire room began to decompress.

Archer was yanked over the railing where he held on for dear life watching the doors open on the stunning sight of the stellar nursery. In the struggle to maintain his grip on the rail, the phase device resting on his finger was ripped off and sucked into space. Archer could only watch as Silik decamouflaged by the bay doors and leaped into space, dropping down to the awaiting Suliban vessel. Silik had escaped, but at least Archer could take some satisfaction in the fact that the Suliban did not take the futuristic technology with him.

Chapter 8

Archer opened his eyes and found himself lying in darkness once again. This time, however, his conscious mind recognized the shifts in reality. Without being able to see, he knew that he was back in his quarters aboard *Enterprise*.

Was it a dream? he asked himself. His body felt rested, but his mind was wide awake. He wondered if that meant that only his conscious mind had traveled through time. Maybe his body had remained behind, asleep. Looking over at the clock display, he noted that it had been a couple hours since he had first gone to bed. That didn't really tell him anything. Listening closely, he could hear the soft, shallow breathing of a sleeping Porthos.

His mind was filled with the information that Daniels had given him as well as the questions and doubts every word had raised. *But Daniels is dead,* he reminded himself. *Trip saw it happen.*

Pushing past the doubts and the memories of his previous interaction with Daniels and Silik, Archer sat up in his bed. He could not ignore what Daniels had just told him—ten months ago. Forgetting anything else that had happened in the past, he knew it was the only explanation for the recent events, and right now, that was all Archer cared to know.

The only way to discover the truth was to act on the information he'd been given, so Archer hit the lights and sprung out of his bunk. Throwing on his uniform with a renewed sense of determination, he hit the companel on his desk. "All senior staff report to the situation room in fifteen minutes. Mister Reed, I'd like you in my quarters immediately."

Apparently Reed had taken the command very seriously, because the lieutenant was at Archer's quarters in just under a minute. The captain suspected that Reed hadn't been asleep when he received the call, as evidenced by the exhausted look of despair on his face. His uniform seemed slightly crumpled as if he had been lying in it. Archer silently cursed himself from not noticing the lieutenant's obvious guilt-ridden state long before. *But that would have meant dealing with my own issues,* he thought regretfully.

"Malcolm?" he asked as the lieutenant stepped into the quarters.

"Did you find something, sir?" The look on Reed's face was begging for a positive answer.

"Possibly." Archer didn't want to build false hopes, but

he could not contain his own optimistic attitude. "But I'm going to need your help to prove it."

He watched as Reed's entire body came to life. The nearly despondent officer who had come to his door was gone and replaced by a man with renewed purpose. Archer couldn't help but think that all it took was one simple phrase. *No,* he corrected himself, *not just a simple phrase—a command from his captain, who has been wallowing in his own depression for far too long.*

Archer detailed what he needed Reed to do as the pair stepped out onto E-deck, splitting in two directions. While Reed headed for the launch bay, Archer made his way to the bridge. He was almost disappointed that the hour was so late. With hardly any of the crew walking the corridors, he had no one to greet and let know that he was back to his old self. As he rode the turbolift to the bridge, it stopped on B-deck where T'Pol stepped in.

"T'Pol," he said in greeting, maintaining the proper air of dignity expected of a commanding officer.

"Captain," she replied. "May I ask what is so important that it couldn't wait until morning?"

He knew she was throwing his own words back at him. "I've stopped feeling sorry for myself," he cryptically replied as the turbolift opened on the bridge.

Stepping out, he found Trip already waiting. *Is anyone on this ship getting sleep?* he wondered.

"Sir?" Trip asked.

"In the situation room." Archer nodded and moved to

the aft section of the bridge. He stood, silently, not wanting to reveal too much information until the confirmation he was waiting for came in. The night shift crew just looked on, wondering why the senior staff was arriving several hours early.

Minutes later Ensigns Sato and Mayweather came off the turbolift and joined the rest of the staff in the situation room. Archer took his place at the head of the table as the others circled around.

"We're waiting for Malcolm," he announced to his staff.

"Is something wrong, sir?" Trip asked.

"Yeah, something's very wrong," he said, though there was a slight grin on his face for the first time in a while. "But we're about to make it right."

Where's Malcolm? he wondered, pacing with anticipation. *He's got to find it.*

The turbolift doors opened and all heads turned to find Reed entering the bridge, looking slightly confused. Cupped in his hand he carried some kind of small alien component.

Archer knew exactly what it was.

"It was just where we detected the EM signature." Reed held up a round object that was only a few centimeters in diameter. "But I don't understand. It was completely invisible. How on earth did you know that a phase-discriminator would expose it?"

Archer took the component from Reed. It was the first validation of what Daniels had told him. "If I'm not mistaken"—he handed the item to T'Pol—"you'll find this thing was designed to generate a plasma stream."

She kept her eyes on the captain as unspoken questions filled her gaze.

Archer set himself in motion around the table. The energy he had lacked in the past two days suddenly came back and needed an outlet. "Put a team together, Trip. I'll need two quantum beacons. They'll have to be positron-based and have an output of two hundred gigawatts apiece."

"Positron based, sir?" Trip asked to clarify what he had just heard.

Archer knew it sounded like he was requesting the impossible. "Just get started. I'll bring you the specs in a few minutes." He came to Hoshi. "We're going to need our com frequencies on the fritz for a day or so. See to it."

"Aye, sir," she replied, though with much uncertainty in her voice. She knew what he was asking her to do, but she was unclear on the "why."

Archer came back to Reed. "Put the armory on full alert." He knew that they would be seeing action before long. Then he turned to Mayweather. "Turn the ship around, Travis. We're going back to the Paraagan colony."

The crew stared at him, hoping for more.

"What are you all waiting for?"

The officers swung into action as they went to their stations for an early reprieve of the night shift. Trip, however, hung back a little to stay by his friend.

"Sir?" he asked, baffled by the commands.

"It wasn't us, Trip," Archer said, anticipating the question. "We didn't do it."

The captain's change in attitude invigorated Trip as he let out the breath it seemed as if he had been holding in since he discovered the mission was canceled.

Archer knew exactly how he felt.

Chapter 9

In the hours that followed, *Enterprise* was bustling with activity, though most of the crew was not entirely sure of what was going on. Even those in the know had little idea what exactly they were doing. Captain Archer was the only one with all the information, and even he was treading on unknown ground as he moved around the ship bringing each part of the plan together. He knew that every one of his bridge officers would have to play a part, but, more important, he knew that he could count on each and every one of them. In the many months they had spent together, Archer had formed a bond with his crew, one that he regretted letting slip for the past two days. It was now his turn to make up for the missed time.

The entire engineering crew had been called to duty and were waiting for their orders as Archer and Trip huddled in a work area set off from main engineering. The captain was using the information provided by Daniels to explain just what those orders would be. Looking over a wall monitor, Archer quickly detailed the specifications of what he would need the team to create for him.

"Take a look at the dispersal curve." He pointed Trip's attention to the monitor as the image shifted one-hundred-eighty degrees. "Here and here. You'll have to isolate the subassembly tolerances from the emitter algorithms."

"Whoa, hold on a minute." Trip had a perplexed look on his face. "You're saying the assembly's independent of the emitters?"

"Exactly."

"That's impossible."

"Not if you generate a stable flux between the positronic conductors." Archer was aware that even though Trip had more experience and knowledge than anyone on the crew, the words coming out of his mouth probably sounded like little more than technological babble to the engineer. Archer slid his hand across the monitor at a diagonal, illustrating his point. "Then all you'll have to do is renormalize the tertiary wave functions."

"With all due respect, sir"—Trip chose his words carefully—"this is a level of quantum engineering that's beyond anything *I* ever learned. How the hell do you know this?"

Archer finally slowed for a moment, knowing that it was important that Trip believed what he was about to say. His friend was the most likely member of the crew to go along with the plan once he knew where it came from. If Trip balked at this point, Archer was going to need to seriously reconsider how he proceeded. "You remember Crewman Daniels?"

"Yeah." Trip couldn't see where this was going. "I saw him get vaporized by our friend, Silik."

"Well, for a cloud of vapor he's one wealth of information," Archer responded after moving to another monitor to work. "I just spent two hours with him."

"He's on *Enterprise?*" Trip was confused.

"Not exactly," Archer said, well aware of the fact that his nonanswers were becoming very much like Daniels's unclear responses. "Listen, I'll explain later. Right now we've got to get back to building these beacons."

"Whatever you say." Trip was still trying to keep up. But he did keep going, which pleased Archer immeasurably.

Archer continued to work with the commander on the development of the beacons until Trip was far enough along that he could finish things up with his engineering team and set about building the devices.

From there the captain headed for the bridge to brief T'Pol and Hoshi on their part of the plan. The trio gathered around the science station in discussion as Mayweather listened in from his station at the helm.

"The circuitry in there isn't compatible with our technology," Archer said, referring to the device T'Pol was still examining. "We're going to have to create an interface."

"What for?" Hoshi asked.

He informed both of them of the riskiest part of the plan. "We're going to be retrieving some Suliban data discs. I have no doubt you'll be able to handle the content. But before you can do that, we'll have to find a way to access the data."

T'Pol continued to examine the component. "And Daniels claimed this is Suliban technology?"

"Everything he has told me has checked out so far," he explained defensively, sensing Vulcan cynicism in her question. "I have no reason to doubt him on this."

"We'll do our best, Captain," Hoshi promised.

The meeting ended and Archer headed for the turbolift for the next phase of the plan.

"Captain," T'Pol stopped him before he was gone. "The Vulcan ship we were headed for . . . it's no doubt detected that we've altered course."

"Have they tried to hail us?" he asked Hoshi.

"I wouldn't know, sir," she said with a small glimmer in her eye. "Our com is on the fritz."

Archer smiled at his com officer before stepping into the turbolift. He was pleased that everything seemed to be going along smoothly, since it would only get more dangerous from here on out.

The turbolift deposited Archer back on E-deck where he met up with Lieutenant Reed. The pair went on to retrieve one of the key elements in the plan and, he hoped, further proof that Daniels could be trusted.

"Why did Daniels leave it in his quarters?" Reed asked as they moved through the corridors. He had brought along the hand-scanner as Archer had requested.

"I don't recall him having much time to pack before he left," Archer wryly commented.

"Well, if it is there," Reed said, "and it contains what he said it does, it could be invaluable to Starfleet."

Archer could understand Reed's enthusiasm, but he had already explained why that was not a part of the plan. "I gave Daniels my word, Malcolm. We download the schematics for the Suliban *stealth*-cruiser. Nothing else."

"Pity," Reed said as they turned a corner and reached Daniels's former quarters where the mag-lock was still in place on the door. After the events of six months ago Archer had ordered Daniels's former roommate shifted to other quarters and the room sealed until such time as it became necessary that it be reopened. Now was that time.

"Assuming he's right and we manage to find the cruiser," Reed said, his tactical mind working, "what makes you think the Suliban won't come after us?"

"Just like those old Bible movies, Malcolm. 'It wasn't written.' "

Archer watched as Reed keyed in the combination to the mag-lock. The red light changed to green as the magnetic force of the lock shut down and Reed removed it from the door. Archer took a deep breath as they stepped into the darkened quarters. He had often considered exploring the room to see what kind of treasures it could be holding, but he knew how dangerous it would be to mess with technology supposedly nine hundreds years ahead of their time. Now that he was going in there on a specific mission, he couldn't help but feel both excitement and apprehension.

As light spilled in from the corridor, Archer opened Daniels's locker and reached for the upper compartment. Brushing aside a folded article of clothing, he found the object he was looking for underneath. As Reed turned on an overhead light, Archer moved the metal container over to the deck and set it down, taking a seat himself.

Opening the box, he found a futuristic-looking device. "So far, Daniels is batting a thousand."

Removing the device from the container, Archer examined it for a moment, turning it over in his hands to see where the controls were placed. Reed took a seat on the bunk beside the captain and peered over his shoulder as Archer set the device back down and activated it.

A holographic page shot up from the instrument, pulling Reed off the bunk to stare with curiosity at the wondrous image. Archer tried to get accustomed to the controls as data filled the page floating in front of them.

"What a minute," Reed said, eyeing the text. "Did you see that? They've got schematics on half a dozen Klingon ships!"

Gaining familiarity with the controls, Archer began to scroll through the pages quickly. "The *stealth*-cruiser, Lieutenant. Nothing else."

But as the images flew by, even the captain couldn't help but notice some of the numerous varieties of ships, including a few that seemed as if they could have evolved from *Enterprise* design.

"There! There it is," Reed said as the image flashed before them.

Hitting another control, Archer made the rest of the page disappear as a three-dimensional schematic of the Suliban ship was pulled out and hung in front of them. He motioned to Reed, who took out the hand-scanner and moved it slowly across the floating image. Archer waited while the scanner absorbed the data, ticking off each new clue as further proof that Daniels could be trusted.

With the information in hand, Archer placed the futuristic device back in its casing and returned it to the locker, figuring this would be the safest place on the ship to store it for the time being, since only he and Reed were aware of its specific contents. They returned to the corridor and placed the mag-lock back on the door.

"Download the information into the tactical computer," Archer instructed. "And plot out the attack plan."

"Aye, sir," Reed replied as he headed for the armory.

Archer returned to engineering, where he found Trip working with his team fine-tuning the two large particle beacons that were sitting on the deck. Even though Archer had provided the specifications, they were unlike anything he had ever imagined.

He looked over the strange devices as he made his way through the workstation. "Trip?"

"I feel like a chef who's just made a meal with ingredients he's never tasted," he said, moving back to his work.

"You followed the instructions?"

"To the letter."

Archer moved over to examine one of the devices more closely.

"Bridge to Captain Archer," T'Pol's voice came over the com system.

Archer tapped a nearby companel. "Go ahead."

"We're approaching the colony," she replied via com.

"Have Mister Mayweather locate a binary system two point five light-years away and set a course," he instructed.

"Understood," she responded, ending the transmission.

Energized that his plan was coming together, Archer headed back toward the corridor. "Let's get these mounted on the grappler arms," he said, giving one final instruction before leaving Trip to finish the job.

Stepping out into the hall, he resisted the temptation to find a port and look out at the charred planet they had returned to. He felt a twinge of guilt bubble up once again over the lives that had been lost only two days ago. This time, it wasn't guilt borne out of responsibility, but regret over the fact that he had not spent the time to properly mourn the losses of the colonists. He had been so wrapped up in blaming himself for what had happened that the never guided his crew in a properly respectful service in honor of the Paraagans. Although he was aware that this was not the day for such a ceremony, he made a mental note to himself to come back at a proper time.

Soon after, *Enterprise* was flying at impulse, approaching two stars linked together by plumes of glowing hydrogen. On the bridge Archer was pleased to see more and more of Daniels's information being confirmed.

"Head for the smaller star," he instructed Mayweather. "Then the inner moon of the second planet."

Mayweather nodded in response and worked the helm, inputting the captain's directions.

Archer hit a button on the companel built into the helm. "Bridge to armory."

"Reed here," came the reply.

"Have you plotted all the target points?"

Down on F-deck, Reed was looking over a two-dimensional version of the Suliban *stealth*-cruiser schematic on his workstation as tactical crewmen were busy loading torpedoes into the launch tubes. "Aye, sir."

"Stand by," Archer instructed from the bridge.

On the viewscreen a small barren moon could be seen looming larger as they moved the ship closer. Archer looked to Trip and T'Pol. "I'll meet you two in the launch bay. If this goes well, I shouldn't be long." He didn't want to think about their options if the early part of the plan *didn't* succeed.

T'Pol and Trip headed for the turbolift as Archer turned his direction back to Mayweather. "Lower the beacons."

The ensign worked the controls, lowering the grappling arms into place. The end of each arm was fitted with the beacons that had been installed by the engineering team, replacing the clamps that had been used to retrieve Shuttlepod One just days ago.

Pressing the controls on his command chair, a monitor popped up from the arm. He tapped a few buttons, transferring information from his computer to Hoshi's station. "Modify the viewscreen," he instructed her, "and bring up these coordinates. Full magnification."

Hoshi worked the controls, and the viewscreen moved in to a closer display of the moon, focusing on a rocky outcropping on the surface.

"Activate the beacons," he said to Mayweather, who did as commanded.

Slowly a shadow of green appeared in front of them. It was in the same flat design with a horseshoe-shaped bow as the schematic provided by Daniels's device. The Suliban ship was attached to a small docking structure hovering above the rocky outcropping. Both the ship and docking structure were somewhat transparent as the beacons revealed them to be cloaked.

Archer eyed the image, satisfied and determined. "Right where they're supposed to be."

"Aren't we in range of their sensors, sir?" Hoshi asked with concern, but not fear.

"They can see us," he confirmed. "But they have no idea we can see through their cloak." But Archer knew that didn't mean they should lower their guard. "Just keep on the same course, Travis."

Tension rose as they watched the viewscreen.

Waiting.

Archer tapped the companel. "Malcolm?"

"The closer the better, sir."

The Suliban ship loomed ever close on the viewscreen. After a long tense beat an alarm at Hoshi's station broke through the silence. "They're charging weapons!" she announced.

Archer returned to the companel. "Now, Mister Reed." Without waiting for a reply, he turned and went for the turbolift.

As the captain made his way to the launch bay, *Enterprise* let loose a barrage of fire from the two forward phase canons. The Suliban ship was hit by the programmed precision strikes at various points in the hull. Each phase blast illuminated the vessel as the ship's cloak fritzed. After a half dozen hits the cloak blew out and the ship was fully revealed.

In the armory Reed and his crew were at work. The lieutenant's eyes were glued to the schematic of the Suliban cruiser, which had glowing red blips indicating the damage as it was inflicted.

"Their cloaking generator's down," a tactical crewman to his side confirmed.

"All four weapons banks as well," Reed noted.

They kept working as outside the ship, the Suliban *stealth*-cruiser was hit by another series of precisely targeted phase-cannon strikes.

"Port and starboard engines disabled," the crewman went on to report.

"Okay," Reed acknowledged as he continued to align the weaponry. "Here's the tricky part."

Focusing the battle, a single phase-canon blast struck a lower section of the Suliban hull. It was now safe for the captain to proceed.

Reed eyed the schematic, confirming the damage, and tapped the companel. "Reed to Shuttlepod Two."

In the launch bay Trip was at the helm of the shuttle-pod, with T'Pol in a jumpseat behind him. Archer had just made it inside and was pulling the hatch closed behind him. "Archer here," he said into the com.

"She's all yours, Captain," Reed's voice came over the system. "Good luck."

Upon hearing the go-ahead, Trip drop-launched the shuttle, flying it toward the moon and the Suliban ship.

Chapter 10

"That last shot should've sealed off the two lower decks." Archer took three phase pistols from the weapon's locker, handing one to T'Pol, who was looking over the cruiser schematic on a padd. He kept the other two for himself and Trip. "If Daniels was right, there shouldn't be more than twenty Suliban for us to deal with."

"Is that all?" Trip sarcastically asked, piloting the shuttle.

The pod carefully made its way to the Suliban cruiser, dropping beneath the alien ship. Toward the middle of the vessel, Trip edged the shuttlepod up to the docking port, easing its way up before clamping onto the port with the exterior hatch.

Moving through the docking port into the Suliban ship, Archer slid aside a small hexagonal hatch in the floor of a room with similar hatches on the walls and ceiling. Armed with their phase-pistols Archer and T'Pol climbed up into the room first. Stepping to the controls of the main wall hatch, Archer confirmed information on his padd and punched a code Daniels had given him into the wall unit.

He turned to see that Trip had also ascended from the shuttle with his phase pistol ready as well as two Starfleet-issue stun grenades—one attached to the belt on his waist and the other in his hand. Poised by the controls to the wall hatch, Archer nodded to the commander that he was ready.

"The stun grenade's on a three-second delay," Trip said in a hurried whisper as he activated the grenade with its pulsing blue light and high-pitched whine.

Archer tapped one last command into the controls, and the hexagonal wall hatch slid open to reveal a seemingly empty corridor. Trip quickly tossed the grenade through the hatch as the three of them jumped back within the airlock chamber to shield themselves from the coming blast.

The stun grenade clattered across the deck and released a blinding concussive blast that briefly lit up the darkened gray corridor. The flash revealed several camouflaged Suliban clinging to the walls and ceiling, lying in wait, but the force of the blast dropped them to the deck, unconscious, and visible.

Archer fell to one knee at the threshold, aiming his weapon into the corridor. Confirming that the area was clear, he cautiously stepped through the hatch with T'Pol and Trip quickly following, phase pistols at the ready.

As the hatch sealed shut behind them, T'Pol consulted her padd and nodded in the direction of the corridor in front of them. They started down the darkly lit hall, moving past the fallen Suliban soldiers. Archer had never been in a Suliban cruiser before, but the interior was reminiscent of the cell-ships in which he had once had the unfortunate circumstance of being trapped. The dim blue lighting made it all the better for the Suliban to hide.

On the move, the trio wound their way through the maze-like gray metal passageways with the familiar hexagonal designs on the walls and floor. T'Pol followed the schematics map that Reed had downloaded onto her padd and, reaching another intersection, she pointed them to the right and down an adjoining corridor.

Before they could move, however, Suliban weapons fire flashed through the hall behind them, hitting a nearby bulkhead. The team split from Archer in the right corridor and T'Pol and Trip diving to the left. Without pausing, Archer spun back toward the corridor from which they had come and laid down covering fire as his officers crossed the open intersection unscathed and continued down the corridor. Once he confirmed they were safe, he fell in behind them.

From the *Enterprise* armory, Reed watched moving representations of his crewmates on the monitor at his workstation. He highlighted a section of schematic and a representation of the cruiser's interior came up with three blips representing the captain, commander, and subcommander.

"Just ten more meters," Reed said, wishing that he was on the cruiser with them instead of just watching over them.

With Suliban in front of them and behind, the trio rushed down the dimly lit passageways as weapons blasts buzzed over their heads. Firing back, they cleared the halls as they neared their ultimate destination. Rounding yet another corner, they finally came to the room they had been searching for—the ship's computer core.

Archer paused to confirm that the route to the room was clear. "Go!" he urged them as they moved toward the room in concert with one another. As the hatch opened, Archer stepped though first, quickly followed by the others.

The chamber was filled with computer stations, banks of complex Suliban graphics filling the screens. A roiling mass of energy swirled along one wall. As Archer and T'Pol went into the heart of the room, Trip took up position by the doorway. Activating another stun grenade, he flung it out into the hall to give them some time. The force of the grenade knocked out their pursuers as it briefly lit the computer room.

"Which one?" T'Pol asked as she checked the various stations.

Archer quickly climbed a ladder to the upper deck to consult the computer core itself for the location of the specific terminal they needed. "Here." He jumped back down to the main level and took a seat at the station farthest from the entryway.

Looking over the panel, he tried to recall the information that Daniels had provided him. There had already been so many aspects of the plan that it was beginning to get a little overwhelming. Carefully he tapped a sequence of controls and was rewarded by the sound of several servos disengaging.

A small section of the console slid open to reveal a jumble of Suliban circuitry and a collection of data discs. Eyeing the mixture of computer parts, Archer reached in to remove the three translucent data discs he had been sent to retrieve. Slipping them in his pocket, he shot T'Pol a look of satisfaction.

Suliban soldiers were rushing toward them, dropping through the ceiling and coming up through floors as the trio hurried back to the shuttlepod, following the circuitous path they had already taken. They managed to stay ahead of their pursuers until they reached another intersection, where T'Pol checked her padd to find that they were no longer alone.

"Captain, they're all around us," T'Pol said, betraying no emotion.

The screen showed half a dozen Suliban were coming at them. But what it could not show was that some of the determined soldiers were crawling along the walls and ceilings as others hurried, crouched beneath them. The genetically enhanced soldiers were moving fast and would overtake Archer, Trip, and T'Pol at any moment.

Taking position behind a bulkhead, Archer flipped open his handheld communicator. "Archer to Reed."

"Go ahead," the lieutenant's voice shot back.

"We could use a little help here," he said, though his calm voice was not in keeping with the tense situation.

Reed checked his scanner and watched as the blips moved through the ship. "I see them." He worked on the controls. The beacons had not only included the technology to reveal the cloaked ship, but they also helped in displaying the positions of Suliban on the ship. The enemy appeared on Reed's monitor as red blips as opposed to the Starfleet blue. This technology went far beyond the powers of the sensor device that Daniels had introduced to the crew during their last encounter.

Confirming the readout, Reed aimed the phase cannon at the starboard section of the cruiser and fired. A bolt of energy shot out from *Enterprise*, hitting directly on target and destroying part of the Suliban ship.

The *Enterprise* team had braced themselves against the wall, as the ship rocked from the explosion. The corridor to their right imploded, sending the Suliban flying, engulfed by the debris.

Archer, T'Pol, and Trip remained hunkered down against the wall as the shaking from the blast subsided. Once they saw their path was now clear of their pursuers, they made their way back into the intersection, turning left into the opposing corner.

Returning to the airlock chamber, Archer opened the wall hatch and Trip dashed inside first to clear it of Suliban, but found that it was empty. Without stopping, he opened the deck hatch leading back down to the shuttle-pod and began climbing down into the pod.

Archer moved to the controls for the wall hatch and was punching in commands when a Suliban lunged at him. The hatch slid shut, blocking the soldier from entering behind them.

T'Pol began to make her way down the ladder as Archer reached her, lending a hand to help guide her back into the ship. Once she was safely inside, Archer descended into the pod, closing the hatch behind him. Working the controls of the pod, Trip readied for their departure as the others took their jumpseats.

Above them, a pair of Suliban soldiers forced their way into the airlock chamber. Working at the control panel, they commanded the hatch in the floor to slide away and dropped down the port onto the hull of the escaping shuttlepod.

Inside the shuttle, the *Enterprise* team could hear the sound of the docking mechanism straining to disengage as the pod tried to pull away from the ship. The shuttlepod would not fly.

"What's the problem?" Archer asked.

"I can't release the docking clamps," Trip said, still working.

"Ignite the thrusters," the captain ordered.

A banging noise came from above, drawing their attention to the ceiling. T'Pol drew her phase pistol and took position beneath the hatch, preparing to fire if the Suliban managed to breach the ship. More thumping and scratching could be heard as the Suliban tried to force their way inside the craft. Then the entire shuttle began to shudder as the thrusters strained against the powerful docking clamps.

Archer ordered a risky maneuver. "Go to full power!"

Following the captain's orders, Trip pushed the shuttlepod to maximum power and finally wrenched itself away from the cruiser.

As the docking clamps tore away, the Suliban soldiers tumbled out of the port, falling through space. Their genetically altered respiratory systems allowed them to remain conscious as they dropped toward the moon, caught in the slight gravitational pull as they fell to their probable deaths.

Shuttlepod Two was still trembling from the violent launch as Trip's fingers danced over the controls steering them back to *Enterprise*. The pod rapidly ascended from the moon allowing the team to take a moment to breathe and enjoy the success of their victory, secure in the knowledge that the Suliban were not going to follow.

Archer was relieved that they had made it and amazed by what they had just done. He tapped the companel on to speak with *Enterprise*. "Archer to Mayweather."

"We see you, Captain," Mayweather's voice came over the com.

"Set a course back toward the Vulcan ship," Archer said, the relief in his voice now obvious. "Go to warp four as soon as we're aboard."

"Yes, sir."

Archer cut off communication with his ship. Taking one of the discs from his pocket, he examined the device. The small data disc seemed so insignificant to look at, but it was all the proof he needed to exonerate himself and his crew.

Chapter 11

"Tell me you have what we're looking for," Archer said as soon as he stepped from the turbolift onto the bridge. It had been a few hours since they had returned from the mission on the Suliban cruiser, and he had been anxiously waiting in his quarters for the call from the bridge. He had wanted to be involved in the decryption of the Suliban data discs, but knew that T'Pol and Hoshi would fare better without him hovering over their shoulders.

"I think you'll be pleased, sir," Hoshi replied as he moved next to her, leaning against a console.

"Was the Suliban language difficult to translate?" he asked, wondering about the delay.

"It ran through the translation matrix perfectly," Hoshi replied. "Once we could read it, that is."

"It took a while before we realized the three discs had to

work in unison," T'Pol explained from her seat at the science station. "The interface seems to be holding."

Archer leaned in, looking over the jury-rigged piece of equipment T'Pol and Hoshi had put together. The three data discs were situated beside each other, seated partially in the device.

"Hoshi?" he asked her to brief him on their findings.

"The *Stealth*-cruiser was definitely in orbit of the Paraagan colony when the explosion took place," she explained, referring to the text she brought up on her screen. "They were monitoring us very closely." She pointed to the display. "There are sensor logs that tracked our course, our altitude, even our hull temperature. Look at this." Tapping another control, the screen shifted from text to imagery as a series of photos of *Enterprise* shot from different angles came up.

"I can't believe how close they got," Archer replied, looking at the images.

"They got a lot closer than you think," T'Pol commented as she joined them at Hoshi's station. Pressing a button, she brought up even more intimate angles of the ship as well as Shuttlepod One as it dropped out of the launch bay. Tapping the key again and again, the frozen images from the cruiser moved closer and closer to the pod.

"These cloaking devices sure come in handy," Hoshi mused.

As T'Pol continued to scan through the images, Archer watched as the cruiser moved in directly beneath the pod and even attached itself to the outer hull under the starboard plasma duct. Archer watched with a combination of anger and vindication as the images continued and the soldiers aboard cruiser eventually finished what they were doing and moved away from the shuttle.

"They were docked with the shuttlepod for nearly two minutes," T'Pol summed up the images.

Archer picked up the Suliban component that Reed had discovered earlier. "Just long enough to attach this and cloak it." With practically a spring in his step, Archer moved toward his ready room. "Good work. Keep at it. And get me Admiral Forrest."

His tension headache had not abated since the first meeting with the Command Council. Now Admiral Forrest was in his tenth such meeting in two days. This time, however, he was busy trying to explain to his peers that *Enterprise* had not made its rendezvous with the Vulcan ship. Even worse, he knew that Archer was playing games with the Vulcans, pretending that their com system was malfunctioning rather than answering hails. Forrest could only hope that no one else was wise to the trick.

He saw his aide enter the conference room, quickly heading toward him.

"Admiral," the lieutenant whispered into his ear while yet another council member was yelling about something totally off subject.

"Not now," he replied through grit teeth.

But the lieutenant knew better than to be swayed by the admiral's ire. *"Enterprise* is trying to contact you."

Forrest shot up from his seat suddenly as the entire council grew silent.

"If you'll excuse me,'" he said, moving toward the door. "There is something I must attend to."

Commander Williams grabbed him before he could go. "What now?" he whispered.

"Nothing," Forrest replied, not wanting to tip his hand before he knew what Archer had been up to while out of contact. "Just update me if I miss anything important."

"That is highly doubtful," Williams replied with an exasperated sigh.

Once again hurrying through the halls of Starfleet Headquarters, Forrest returned to his office to find Archer's image already waiting for him on his viewscreen.

"Jonathan, where the hell have you been?" he asked before he had even sat in his chair.

"Sorry we had to disappear for a while, Admiral," Archer replied. "But I think you'll be happy with the reason."

"I should hope."

"What would you say if I could prove *Enterprise* was not the cause of the tragedy at the Paraagan Colony?" Archer asked.

"I'd say prove it." The admiral was not in the mood for banter. He wanted facts.

Captain Archer then proceeded to detail those facts, explaining in great detail exactly what proof he had of *Enterprise*'s innocence. Forrest couldn't believe what he was hearing. Suddenly a slew of additional meetings was going to be added to his schedule, but this time he knew he would enjoy them. *Well, most of them.* He silently wondered if he could make it back in time to the Command Council meeting before the yelling got so out of hand that they ending the gathering in disgust.

"Sounds like pretty solid evidence," Forrest said, trying to maintain his optimism until he actually saw the images himself. "Where the hell did you get it?"

The captain was nearly beaming. "It's all on three data discs we took from a cloaked Suliban ship."

The amazement continued. "How did you know about that cruiser?" Forrest asked. "And if it was cloaked, how did you find it?"

"I've got friends in high places," Archer replied with a grin.

"This is going to be a very interesting briefing," Forrest replied, looking forward to the report. "Get to the Vulcan ship as quickly as you can. I'll let them know what you've got."

There was a hesitation on the other end of the com. "That Vulcan ship was sent to pick up T'Pol and Doctor Phlox," Archer reminded the admiral, "not to help us vindicate ourselves."

"Those discs are hard evidence," Forrest replied, determined. "Once the Vulcans see them, they'll have no choice but to reconsider their recommendations." Then he moved on to a more pleasant subject. "I can't tell you how pleased I am, Jonathan. After all that you've done, I would have hated to see this end."

"Thank you for believing in us, Admiral," Archer replied, sitting a little taller. "Archer out."

The screen blinked off in front of the Admiral. It was just the kind of communiqué he had needed to receive. He knew that he had been speaking slightly out of turn when he told the captain that the hard evidence would convince the Vulcans. That was still an unknown entity. The Vulcans certainly didn't make decisions for the Command Council, but their influence, unfortunately, held a lot of weight. As the initial exuberance passed, Forrest realized that there was still much work to be done.

Light-years away from Earth, another briefing was taking place. This one, however, was not over a great distance so much as it was occurring over a tremendous amount of time.

Hidden within a deep red nebula, the massive Suliban Helix hung safely away from their enemies. The alien space station was comprised of hundreds of cell-ships interlocked together. Deep within its twisting corridors, Silik, the leader of the Suliban Cabal, was busy updating his mysterious benefactor from the future on recent events.

Inside the temporal chamber, time moved differently, layered with a pre-echo effect as two different centuries met as one. The humanoid figure stood within a barrier of rippling energy, shifting in and out of reality, never long enough to take definite shape and reveal his true identity. Facing him, Silik stood in a circle of light, addressing the mysterious being, assuming that the projection of his image must appear similarly distorted centuries in the future.

"They boarded cloaked vessels," Silik said, already adopting a defensive tone. "And they knew exactly where to find the discs."

"They weren't acting alone," the figure calmly explained.

But Silik knew the figure did not accept failure. He needed to find a way to make amends before he was punished. "My ships are fast. We can overtake them . . . destroy *Enterprise*."

"Have your ships bring me Archer," he replied. "Allow *Enterprise* to continue."

"But we need to recover the discs," Silik insisted.

"*Archer*," the figure said, adopting an ominous tone. "You know what happened the last time you failed me." The being disappeared immediately following the threat as the chamber returned to normal time.

Silik had remembered the punishment quite well. His future benefactor had been generous with his gifts of genetic enhancements to the Suliban. But Silik had made the mistake of considering them gifts instead of loans bartered against his services. For the mysterious figure had the power to take away as well as to give. Silik's first failure when dealing with the *Enterprise* crew and Jonathan Archer had cost him with the painful extraction of his enhanced vision. Additional failures would lead to the removal of more of the gifts. And Silik knew without a doubt that once all the enhancements were removed, he would pay for whatever final failure with his life.

Chapter 12

"It was ten months ago," Archer insisted. "He brought me back *ten months*. But I knew everything I know now. How is that possible?"

Standing in the captain's ready room, T'Pol did not looked convinced. "As I've told you, the Vulcan Science Directorate has concluded that time travel is impossible."

"Well, good for the Vulcan Science Directorate," Archer replied, dripping with sarcasm. "Maybe they can tell me how I woke up yesterday knowing exactly where that Suliban ship was. Or how I suddenly had the ability to construct a quantum beacon to see through its cloak. And while they're at it, they might as well tell me how I knew where to find those discs."

It was the first time Archer had to really stop and think things through since his meeting with Daniels. Everything else since then had been about finding the proof to clear his crew. Now that Admiral Forrest had been brought into the loop, Archer finally had the time to consider the full scope of all that he had been through in the past twenty-four hours. For the moment he was pleased that T'Pol refused to keep an open mind about the situation as talking it out with her helped further cement the argument in his own mind. But as he became more and more sure of things, he needed her to go along as well.

"All valid questions." T'Pol's lack of emotion, however, only served to make Archer's outburst seem even more intense. "But to conclude that the only answer is that you acquired this information from a dead crewman who transported you back through time is illogical."

"Then why don't you give me another explanation?" Archer asked, truly wanting one, but knowing he was pushing her too hard. *It isn't her fault my argument goes against decades of indoctrination to believe the Science Directorate without question,* he thought.

"I can't," she simply replied.

"Because there isn't one. I got a call from Trip—something about inspection pods. It was the exact same call I got the day before they found Klaang. Word for word!"

"Perhaps you were dreaming," she suggested, since even he had admitted that the conversation with Daniels had occurred in the middle of the night while he lay in bed.

Archer finally softened his tone. "Listen, I never thought this was possible, either. But I traveled through time and I need you to believe me."

"Why?" T'Pol asked, confused by the sentiment.

Archer tried to explain to the emotion-suppressing Vulcan the purely emotional reason. "Because it's hard enough trying to fathom all this without having my science officer . . . a colleague I trust and rely on . . . the person who got me to stop feeling sorry for myself . . . accusing me of being a hallucinating madman." His body relaxed upon admitting the words.

"I don't remember accusing you of anything," T'Pol said, missing the point entirely.

Archer gave up, with a sigh of frustration.

"Bridge to Archer," Reed's voice came over the com.

With relief over their conversation being brought to an end, Archer tapped the companel. "Yes?"

"We're getting some strange readings, sir," Reed replied. "It might not be a bad idea for you to come out here."

Archer knew that when Reed used the double negative it was a sign of trouble. Opening the door, he stepped onto the bridge and T'Pol followed, taking her position at the science station.

"I've taken the liberty of asking Commander Tucker to join us," Reed said as the captain took the command chair.

"What's the problem?" he asked, tapping a button, causing his armchair display to rise from its housing.

"We're having trouble balancing the warp field."

Looking down, Archer reviewed the information Reed had sent to him. "Looks okay to me."

"It's odd." Reed continued running a check on the system. "It will be stable one moment, then for no reason it will go slightly out of alignment."

Across the bridge Hoshi and Mayweather exchanged a silent look of curiosity as Trip entered from the turbolift.

"What are you guys doing to my engines?" he asked, heading for his station.

"The autostabilizers aren't functioning properly." T'Pol tried to confirm Reed's supposition from her own instruments as well.

Trip moved to his monitor. "The computer ran its last diagnostic on them less than ten minutes ago." He reconfirmed the information he already thought he knew. "They look fine."

"Well, they're not," Reed insisted. "We've had to realign the field a dozen times over the last hour." He looked to Mayweather to confirm his statement.

The ensign nodded in response.

Archer's mind was formulating an idea he did not want to consider. He looked to T'Pol, but she did not seem to make the same connection that he had. He could tell, however, that she certainly noticed the look of concern on his face.

He turned to Reed. "Load torpedoes and stand by all weapons." As the crew reacted around him, he looked to Mayweather. "Deploy the beacons, Travis," and then to Hoshi, "Modify the viewscreen and aim the beacons aft."

Hoshi worked the controls at her station, doing as the captain ordered. She looked to him, waiting for the next command. With a silent nod Archer indicated for her to activate the viewscreen.

An aft view of the ship came up, showing six Suliban cell-ships following closely at warp in the now familiar transparent green tint that indicated they were cloaked.

But Archer wasn't finished with his commands, suspecting the worst. "Swing them down," he told Hoshi, "slowly."

Hoshi worked the controls and the angle on the viewscreen tilted downward, moving in concert with the beacons. Six more cell-ships were revealed beneath the others, also maintaining a close distance.

"It looks like we're in a swarm of cloaked bees," Trip commented.

Archer looked to Reed again. "Charge the phase cannons."

Reed nodded and did as instructed when a beep sounded at Hoshi's panel.

"We're being hailed," she said.

"Put it though." Archer wanted to find out what was going on. He had been told the Suliban wouldn't follow. For the first time Daniels's plan was failing them. *Or was that the real plan all along?* He couldn't help but think. *Had Silik been telling the truth all those months ago? Is Daniels as much our enemy as the Suliban?*

Hoshi worked the controls and an image of Silik appeared in place of the cloaked cell-ships.

"I wouldn't advise using your weapons, Jonathan," he said, cockily using the captain's first name as if they were old friends. "Perhaps if we decloak, you'll understand why."

Silik blinked off the viewscreen as his image was replaced by a forward view of space. Ahead of *Enterprise* a dozen cell-ships slowly decloaked as they traveled along matching *Enterprise*'s speed. Hoshi hit the controls to give them a slow three-hundred-sixty-degree view of the ship, revealing that they were surrounded by dozens of enemy vessels.

"Malcolm?" Archer asked.

Reed tore his eyes away from the main viewscreen to check his station. "They're all armed with high-yield particle weapons."

"How many could you take out?" the captain asked, already suspecting he knew the answer.

"Before they opened fire?" Reed spoke with the sound of resignation in his voice. "Not enough, sir."

Archer nodded to Hoshi again and she reestablished communication with Silik.

Once again the Suliban's face filled the screen. "One of my ships is approaching your starboard docking port," he said without ceremony. "I'd like you to board it immediately."

"What do you want with me?" Archer truly wondered. *And why haven't you asked for the discs back?*

"You have five minutes," Silik said. "If you don't comply, I have permission to destroy *Enterprise*."

"How do I know you won't destroy *Enterprise* either way?"

"You have my word, Captain," Silik replied, sounding somewhat genuine. "And you have four and a half minutes left."

Silik's image disappeared once again, replaced by the haunting image of his armada.

In the long moment that followed, Archer considered his options. He wasn't sure whether or not Silik was bluffing, but he knew the risk was too great. *Enterprise* could not survive in a firefight, and the only way he had a chance of figuring out what was going on was by boarding Silik's ship. Daniels had already failed him by telling Archer that they would not be followed. The captain knew that he could not fail his crew.

He turned to T'Pol, resolute in his decision. "I'm placing you in command. I advise you to maintain your present course and speed. I don't know what's going to happen, but try to keep an open mind." He forced a small smile. "Especially when it comes to things the Vulcan Science Directorate says are impossible."

They held a long look.

"I will try," she replied, and he knew she meant it.

"Captain, this is crazy," Trip calmly insisted. "How do you know what they're going to do—"

"T'Pol's in command, Trip," he said, not letting his friend finish. What he was doing was hard enough without a challenge in front of the rest of his officers. "Do whatever you can to help her." He looked around the room one last time. "That goes for all of you."

He met everyone's eyes one by one, trying to give them the strength he knew they already had, finally settling on Hoshi. "Keep an eye on Porthos for me, would you?"

She nodded as he stepped into the turbolift.

"Remember," he added. "No cheese."

Hoshi smiled despite the her building emotions.

The turbolift doors closed on the captain. He could not look back at his crew, feeling as if he had been abandoning them. He stood motionless as the turbolift began its descent, thinking back to the first time T'Pol had taken command of *Enterprise*. It had been during their mission to return Klaang to the Klingon homeworld. At the time, no one in the crew had trusted her, not even himself. Now he couldn't imagine a more suitable member of the crew to leave in charge. At least that was a small consolation as he went to meet whatever it was his fate held.

The lift stopped and the doors hissed open. Turning, he stepped out into a decimated corridor. Shock flowed through his body as he immediately realized he was no longer on *Enterprise*. Looking back, he discovered the turbolift was gone. Wherever he was, he was alone.

The air was thick with decay as he looked down the dark corridor with its charred and twisted walls. The construction seemed both familiar and alien, but certainly different from anything he had seen before. He could hear the distant eerie sound of a heavy wind whistling through the walls. Archer cautiously began to walk toward the noise.

On the *Enterprise* bridge T'Pol had taken the captain's chair, calculating the most logical way to rescue Archer, knowing the only thing she could do was follow his instruction and continue on the way to the Vulcan ship. Once there, she would convince her superiors to bring reinforcements and find the missing captain.

Hoshi's panel beeped once again. Now it was T'Pol's turn to nod to Hoshi, who activated the screen in response.

"Your captain's playing a very dangerous game, Sub-Commander," Silik said as soon as he appeared.

"Game?" she asked, truly unaware of what he meant.

"He has thirty seconds left," Silik continued. "Did he think I wasn't serious?"

T'Pol gestured in Hoshi's direction. The ensign understood the message and cut off the viewscreen. The subcommander then turned to Trip, who was already working at his station.

"The turbolift's on E-deck," he said, referring to the level that had been Archer's destination. "It's empty."

"Where is he?" T'Pol asked.

Trip continued to work. "I'm not reading his biosigns. He must be on the Suliban ship."

T'Pol took a moment, trying to figure out if Silik was leading them into a trap. Knowing she did not have much time, she motioned back to Hoshi, who brought Silik's image back up on the viewscreen.

"Captain Archer is no longer aboard *Enterprise*," T'Pol said. "Perhaps you should check with the vessel you sent for him."

"I thought he was smarter than this," Silik hissed. "He could have saved all your lives. What a waste."

This time Silik tapped his controls and his image blinked off the screen.

"The docked ship is moving away," Mayweather read off his console.

"It's targeting the warp core," Reed added. Then the information on his screen made his blood run cold. "They're *all* targeting the warp core."

Archer continued to move toward the wind, which was whistling loudly around him. Climbing over fallen beams, he made his way carefully through the hall. He approached a large, jagged opening in a wall that had been a window at one time, long ago. Stepping over some more fallen debris, he could see a devastating vista spread out before him. What appeared to have been a large city had been reduced to a post-apocalyptic nightmare.

He was on the high floor of a burnt-out skyscraper. The shells of scorched buildings stretched out as far as the eye could see. The sky was dark and turbulent. He could hardly tell that it was daytime.

Nothing could be heard but the howling wind.

"Ten minutes ago that vista was more beautiful than anything you could imagine." Daniels stepped out from the debris. His voice was flat and dead.

Archer turned to find the man dressed in a black, ribbed uniform with no discernible insignia. He appeared to be nearly as confused as Archer and twice as affected by the devastation around them.

"Where am I?" Archer asked.

Daniels pointed to a nearby doorway, dazed. "I had breakfast in that room less than a half hour ago," he said, partially ignoring the question. "Then I was instructed to bring you here. They told me the timeline wouldn't be safe if you boarded that Suliban ship." Daniels paused to consider what he was saying. "Someone was very mistaken."

"Where is here?"

"You're in the thirty-first century, Captain," he said, answering the *when*, but not the *where*. "Or what's left of it."

"You said the Suliban wouldn't follow us," Archer pressed on, trying to get a straight answer out of Daniels. "That we'd make it safely to the Vulcan ship."

"As far as I was told, that was exactly what was supposed to occur." His voice was still flat.

"So you're telling me this just happened?" Archer looked out at the scene of decimation. "It doesn't look like this just happened."

"No," Daniels replied, trying to figure it out himself. "It looks like it happened a long time ago."

Archer took in what Daniels was saying. "If bringing me here caused this, then send me back. I'll take my chances with Silik."

"You don't understand," Daniels said. "All our equipment . . . the time portals . . . they've been destroyed. *Everything's* been destroyed." He took a deep breath. "There's no way to send you back."

Archer was stunned by Daniels's words. Unable to speak, he stepped forward to view the devastation. Through the haze and smoke he could see dozens of buildings blackened and charred. Rubble covered the streets, but from his vantage point, he could see no people . . . no life at all. The hollow wind continued to blow around him, bringing with it the smell of death and decay.

Chapter 13

The atmosphere on the *Enterprise* bridge could not have been more tense. Members of the crew were conducting various types of internal scans at their stations trying to figure out where their captain had gone. They worked under the watchful eye of Silik as his enraged face filled the viewscreen, thirty Suliban ships continued to aim their weapons at the Starfleet vessel.

"He's not onboard," T'Pol said with an edge of intensity. "You must have sensors that can confirm that."

Silik was losing patience with what he believed to be stalling tactics. "You've lied to me before! If you don't tell me where he is, I'll have no alternative but to . . ."

"Come see for yourself," T'Pol calmly offered, "or send your soldiers. You'll realize I'm telling the truth."

Glances were exchanged around the bridge as the officers silently questioned T'Pol's tactics.

Silik wondered what kind of game the Vulcan was playing and how far she was willing to take it. "Drop out of warp," he commanded, "and prepare to be boarded."

Reed's finger was already hovering over the controls of his console. The moment Silik's image blinked off the viewscreen he tapped the com. "Security teams to docking ports one, two, and three."

T'Pol tapped the com on the command chair in response. "This is Sub-Commander T'Pol," she said ship-wide. "All security teams remain where you are."

Trip jumped out of his seat. "Are you crazy?" he asked, composure gone. "How do we know how many Suliban are coming aboard? They could try to take over the ship."

As usual, T'Pol ignored his highly emotional state and stuck to the facts. "There are thirty armed vessels surrounding us," she reminded the commander. "Unless I'm mistaken, their weapons are targeting our warp core. Mr. Reed?" She looked over to the tactical officer.

The lieutenant checked his console to confirm information he already knew. He acknowledged with a nod of his head.

"So unless you have a better suggestion?" she asked.

Trip hesitated. He wanted to come up with a dozen alternative scenarios, but knew that she was right. They were going to have to wait this one out and see where the Suliban took them figuratively and literally. He shrugged his reluctant agreement to T'Pol as she took a seat in the command chair.

* * *

How the hell did I get here?

The question that Captain Archer asked himself had nothing to do with the temporal mechanics involved in time travel. He wasn't worried about disproving the Vulcan Science Directorate's views on the concept. All that he was concerned about was how the hell he had wound up almost a thousand years in the future.

What exactly was the point of no return?

Archer stepped out of what once was an apartment building and into the desolate street. Daniels had told him that he was in the future, but this was like no future he had ever imagined. The buildings around him were decimated. The ground beneath his feet was pockmarked and laden with rubble. It was as if the future had imploded around him.

He cautiously followed Daniels down a narrow street, careful to keep an eye out for falling debris. With their postapocalyptic exteriors, the buildings looked as though chunks could fall off them at any moment. But this was no recent destruction. The debris that filled the streets was buried in dirt and dust so crusted over by time that the wind could no longer disturb it. While Archer took in the surroundings with understandable disorientation, he couldn't help but notice that Daniels seemed similarly shell-shocked. The man was moving at the mournful pace of a funeral dirge.

"Where are we exactly?" Archer asked. He didn't recognize the place, but if they were hundreds of years in the future, he wouldn't have expected to.

Daniels looked as if he hadn't even heard the question.

Although Archer could not imagine what was going through the man's mind, he knew there were still questions that needed answers. "What was it you told Trip?" he asked, referring back to a conversation from a much earlier time. "Something about Earth still existing?"

"Depending on your definition of Earth," Daniels droned on, repeating the words he had spoken when he had originally revealed himself to the *Enterprise* crew. He had once excelled at careful wordplay devised to avoid altering the timeline with too much information. But, he clearly wasn't in the mood to play those kinds of games at the moment.

"So are we physically on the planet Earth?"

"Right now where we are hardly even exists," Daniels replied, rallying himself from his near catatonic state, to make a token attempt to continue the game. He had done enough damage.

Great, Archer thought. *Am I going to have to wait to see the Statue of Liberty sticking out of the water before I get my answer to that one?*

Archer refused to give in. He wanted answers. "If this place was destroyed as long ago as it seems to have been, what are *you* doing here?" he asked. "You and your 'watchdog' buddies don't exactly fit into all this."

Daniels was losing his patience with Archer. "You're thinking of time travel like we're in some H. G. Wells novel," he brusquely replied. "We're not. It's far more complicated. There's no way for you to understand."

Don't you condescend to me, Archer thought. He might

not be able to understand the specifics, but he was an educated man. The basic rules would be enough to satisfy him. "Try me."

Again, Daniels chose to ignore the captain.

Archer had had enough. He stopped walking and placed his palm against Daniels's chest. Neither of them would be moving until he received some answers. "I realize your little utopia is gone," he said, "and I sympathize. But if you're telling me the truth, if you pulled me nine hundred years into the future"—he indicated the devastation around them—"to *this* future. I think I deserve some answers!"

"I don't have any answers," Daniels said, more frustrated with himself than with Archer. "And you're right. I *shouldn't* be here—which means you shouldn't be here either. But you are. *We* are." Daniels let out a sarcastic laugh and continued walking without worrying whether or not Archer would follow. "We brought you here to protect the timeline," he said, almost to himself. "We did quite a job."

Archer did follow and nearly walked into Daniels when the man turned a corner and stopped without warning. His face registered a peculiar range of emotions, from shock to resignation.

"What's wrong?" Archer asked, surveying the area. He saw nothing but more of the same crumbling buildings they had passed since leaving the apartment building.

"It's gone."

"What's gone?" Archer asked. There didn't look to be

anything missing from the area in front of him. It was just row after row of decay.

"The monument," Daniels replied. "It was right here, on the same street as the library." He seemed to accept the full ramifications of what he was seeing and added it to the list of growing regrets. "It was obviously never built."

The man's reaction triggered yet another in Archer's series of questions. "Why is that a problem?"

No response.

It was beginning to piss the captain off.

"Who did it commemorate?" he asked, pressing for information. *And what did that person have to do with what's going on around us?* he wondered.

"Not who" was Daniels's simple reply.

"Then *what*," he persisted.

"An organization," Daniels replied. His words were tentative. It was as if he didn't want to bring himself to say the words aloud. "A Federation. It doesn't exist for you. Not yet."

"But it will?" Archer wasn't just asking for the sake of clarification. He wanted to know.

Yet, Daniels once again chose not to answer. He seemed preoccupied, which Archer could certainly understand. But that was no reason to shut the captain out of the situation.

"Okay, fine," Archer said, giving up on the useless line of questioning. "Keep your monument to yourself. Where's the library you were talking about?"

Daniels pointed farther down the street. "It should be down there. If it ever existed."

Finally, Archer had a destination. If a library was there,

it was bound to have some kind of information. At the very least, there would be something to tell him where he was—and possibly a more precise answer as to when. He started walking in the direction that Daniels had pointed without bothering to see if the man would follow.

"But even if it is there, it'll be no help," Daniels added as he caught up with the captain. "All the data's stored electronically."

The pair continued walking through the burnt-out city streets in silence. Archer knew that any further conversation would be pointless. He was going to have to figure out what was happening on his own. At the very least he was going to have to gather enough information to force Daniels into admitting some truths about what could have gone wrong and how it can be fixed.

It did not take long for them to reach the library from the spot where the memorial should have stood. The building was still there, although it looked to be in about the same shape as the surrounding environs. Archer stopped at the foot of a huge flight of stone stairs.

"I take it, this is a good thing?" he asked.

"Depends on what we find inside," Daniels responded as he began the ascent up the staircase with Archer in tow.

The captain could make out some writing above the entrance to the library, but years of weather and neglect had wiped away much of the lettering. He couldn't be sure, but it looked to be written in Latin, or possibly Greek. There really weren't enough of the letters left for him to even attempt to translate.

Daniels pushed open the doors blocking the library entrance. They nearly fell off their hinges as the rusted metal gave way under pressure. The creaking sound implied that no one had passed through them for years.

The interior looked as time ravaged as the rest of the city. Archer briefly wondered if the destruction had been limited to this city or did it extend over the entire planet. If this was Earth, it should be teeming with life in every corner of the globe by this point in the future. Surely everyone couldn't be gone from the entire planet. *They just couldn't*, he insisted.

A strong breeze blew through the lobby, kicking up some scraps of paper. Archer knew that it would be hard to determine how long ago the library had been abandoned since it was so exposed to the elements. Then again, he was wasn't sure that it mattered. He just wanted to know how he could get back home.

"Books," Daniels said as they stepped into the library's huge rotunda. "Made with paper. There aren't supposed to be books here."

"Well, there are," Archer stated the obvious. "So I suggest we use some of them to figure out what you did to the last thousand years when you brought me here this morning."

He thought back to the local library that he visited while growing up. His father took him there every other week to teach him about the history of flight. Together they would look over images of da Vinci's designs and the Wright brothers' test flight. They had read all the logs of the first astronauts and watched the vid clips of the first moon landing. It was in that library that his dreams of exploration had been nurtured.

The library he was standing in was a hundred times the size of his library back home, but it reminded him of home nevertheless. Certainly much of the information he had looked at as a child had been stored on computers, but the old book rooms were nowhere near extinction in his time. Daniels's surprise over seeing the books was yet another bit of information that Archer could do nothing with.

Daniels and he moved into the room. The sign above them indicated that they were in the fiction section. *Or, more appropriately, the science fiction section,* he thought. *Well, at least everything's written in English,* he thought. A clue, perhaps, as to where he had been taken.

Archer was tempted to see what books might still be popular in whatever time this library had been abandoned. Maybe this was Earth's future. That possibility was becoming more real to him than it had been a short time ago. That meant he was walking on ground that he should never have set foot upon and seeing things that no one else he knew would ever see. It was as exciting a concept as it was frightening. He was sure that he would have appreciated it more for its educational value if there had even been the slightest hint that he could ever go back to the time in which he belonged.

Chapter 14

Enterprise was dead in space. Dozens of cell-ships hung around it, blocking off any means of escape. Not that the crew was going anywhere. Three of the Suliban vessels had docked with the *Enterprise* and deposited their crews. Suliban soldiers had quickly overrun the ship with teams conducting various scans as well as a physical search of the vessel. T'Pol had been allowed to make a brief announcement to the crew, ordering them to stand down and allow the boarders to proceed, but some members of the *Enterprise* crew were having a difficult time following orders.

A trio of Suliban could not get into Captain Archer's quarters. A snarling four-legged creature guarded the open door. It didn't look particularly vicious to the Suliban, until they considered its teeth, which had been bared. This was the one room they knew needed to be searched and this life-form was not going to stand in their way. The lead Suliban raised his weapon, making sure it was on the "kill" setting.

"Hold on," a woman's voice defiantly called from down the hall.

"Do not interfere," one of the soldiers said, glaring at her.

Crewman Cutler approached the Suliban fearlessly. "He's just a harmless little dog," she said, stepping between the invaders and Porthos. "Nothing to worry about. I'll get him out of your way." She bent to pick up Porthos and take him out of the line of fire.

"See to it that he does not disturb us any further," the lead Suliban ordered as they stepped into the captain's quarters.

"Certainly," she replied, hurrying away with the dog. "Did the big green men scare you?" she asked Porthos once the soldiers were out of earshot.

The dog just growled in response.

"I didn't think so," she giggled. "You could have taken them."

Cutler continued through the halls of E-deck, passing another team of Suliban in the mess hall. They had rows of crewmen lined up against the wall as they tore the place apart. Chef did not look at all happy with the invasion of his kitchen. Luckily the Suliban hadn't seen Cutler as she passed or else she probably would have been pulled in there as well.

The corridors were pretty much empty as she wound her way around the deck. Cutler assumed that most of the crew had taken to their posts. It was one thing to cooperate as T'Pol had ordered, but it was quite another to allow the aliens to run rampant through the ship unchecked. She had been heading for sickbay to look in on the doctor when she had run into Porthos and the Suliban. No telling what the Suliban could do with the collection of serums the doctor held in sickbay.

"What have we got here?" Phlox asked as she entered the room.

"Just another guest," Cutler replied, referring to the collection of fauna that the doctor kept around for medical purposes. "I hate to put him in a cage, but I think it might be in his best interest if we kept him out from underfoot of the Suliban."

"A good idea," the doctor said as he took Porthos from her arms. "I don't have anything free right now that he would be comfortable in, but I think the decontamination chamber would keep him safe while still allowing him room to move."

Phlox deposited Porthos in the chamber, making sure that the environmental controls were set at a comfortable level. Cutler took a bowl out of one of the cabinets and filled it with water. She left it with Porthos and the doctor closed the dog safely into the room.

"How are you holding up?" Cutler asked.

"Well, it's not the first time we've been overrun by uninvited visitors," Phlox said with his trademark smile. "I'm sure we'll be fine."

"At least it keeps you on this ship for a little longer," Cutler added.

"Indeed," Phlox replied, sensing they were about to get into that uncomfortable territory that she seemed to enjoy so much.

The sickbay doors opened and a pair of Suliban entered, breaking the flirtatious tension with more serious unease. Cutler thought she recognized them as part of the group that had been in the mess hall, but they all sort of looked alike to her, at least from a distance.

"Remain where you are," one of the soldiers ordered with his weapon trained on them. Cutler knew it was more a show of strength than an actual threat. They were here to explore and retrieve, not kill.

The other soldier searched the room with his complex scanning device. He passed it over all the objects large enough to conceal something the size of a full-grown man. He stopped once he reached the door to the decontamination chamber.

"I'm reading a life sign in here," he said to his partner. "Very faint."

"Is that where your captain is hiding?" the other officer demanded.

"Certainly not," Phlox quickly replied. "It's just . . ."

"Open the door," the Suliban with the scanner insisted.

Cutler tried not to laugh. It looked to her like Porthos was going to have a taste of Suliban no matter what. "I'm not so sure that's a good . . ."

"Silence!" the armed soldier ordered, glaring at her. "Do as he said."

"You heard the man," Cutler said, smiling at Phlox. She was interested to see how this little scene played out.

"Hey, watch it!" Rostov said as a soldier pushed him roughly against a wall. He shot a look at Crewman Kelly who had been shoved beside him. He could see in her eyes how tempted she was to reach down and take out her weapon. The Suliban saw it first, however, and removed it for her.

This was the first search party the crewman had seen on D-deck. He assumed they were working their way up from the bottom of the ship. Nine soldiers had pushed past them to make their way into engineering while the two others that had actually forced him and Kelly against the wall took up position around the door. It wasn't long before the *Enterprise* engineering team was forced out of the room and lined up in the hall beside them.

"I think we can take the two guards," Kelly whispered to him. "We outnumber them."

"And they outgun us," he said through clenched teeth. "Not to mention their friends giving engineering the once over."

"We have to take back the ship," she insisted.

"Sub-Commander T'Pol ordered us not to interfere," he reminded her. "They'll probably let us go once they figure out the captain isn't on board." He didn't actually believe what he was saying, but he wanted to keep his friend calm.

"What do you think happened to him?" she asked, trying to ignore the noises coming from engineering. It sounded like the Suliban were tearing it apart.

"Beats me," he said. "There's a whole lot of stuff going on here that we're just out of the loop on."

"I don't know whether to be bothered about that or thankful," Kelly replied.

"Probably a little of each," Rostov agreed. He knew that it was the nature of their lower rank to be excluded from some of the more important goings-on of the ship. The senior staff certainly couldn't take the time to brief the crew on every facet of their mission. Although the situation was understandable, it didn't help things when the ship was under attack or the captain turned up missing. But some things just had to be accepted.

One of the armed Suliban came out of engineering, training his sights on the crewmen lined up against the wall.

"Report to your quarters," he ordered. "Now!"

The collection of crewmen reluctantly left engineering behind as they made their way to the turbolift. Rostov could tell that the engineers were reluctant to leave the warp engine in the hands of the Suliban, but there was nothing any of them could do. He and Kelly hung back a little as they moved through the corridors.

"What do you think the odds are that the Suliban are just going to leave once they find out the captain really isn't on board?" Kelly asked.

"Let's just say that's one bet I wouldn't take," he replied. "But I'm sure T'Pol's got the situation under control."

While his men continued to search the ship for Archer, Silik had other more pressing concerns on the bridge. He cordoned off the bridge crew, with guards keeping them in check at the back of the bridge. Silik's attention was focused on the communications officer, while T'Pol looked on from her perch beside the captain's chair. He glanced back to confirm that one of his men was running an analysis on the stolen discs.

"They haven't been duplicated," the soldier reported once his scans were complete.

Silik turned to the women. He trusted his officer's information, but that didn't mean it wasn't time for a little show of strength. He lifted his disruptor and held it to Hoshi's head. "Is he correct?" he asked.

To Hoshi's credit, she didn't play into his game by answering the question. She did her best to hide her feelings as the metal of the disruptor dug into her temple. All of her past fears about space exploration were becoming reality, yet she was handling herself better than she had ever thought she would.

"Don't you believe your scanners?" T'Pol asked, attempting to divert his attention from Hoshi.

"Is he correct?" Silik asked, pressing the disruptor harder against Hoshi's skin.

"We didn't have time to make a copy," Hoshi finally admitted with only the slightest hint of a quiver in her voice.

"Leave her alone!" Trip said, unable to watch any longer. He started toward them, but was stopped when a weapon was shoved in his own face by one of Silik's guards.

"Lower your weapon," Silik calmly instructed the guard as he removed his own disruptor from Hoshi's forehead. He turned his attention to T'Pol. "If we find Captain Archer aboard this vessel, you'll all be punished for lying to me."

T'Pol refused to break the Suliban's stare.

The turbolift doors opened, releasing Suliban Commander Raan onto the bridge. Armed soldiers flanked the commander as he reviewed the information on the hand scanner he held in front of him.

Silik turned to the commander, expectantly.

"He's not here. Unless he's dead," Raan reported, handing the scanner to his leader. "But we did find this."

Silik eyed the readings with concern. "Where?"

"In that lift," Raan indicated behind him. "It's an hour old. Maybe two."

Silik shifted his attention back to T'Pol. "When I saw him last, your captain spoke of a"—he pretended to search for the words as if he were not already familiar with them—" 'Temporal Cold War.' What was he talking about?"

T'Pol had no interest in playing Silik's game. She kept her answer simple and precise, yet intentionally misleading. "The Captain believed Crewman Daniels was from the future. But if I recall, you killed him."

"What else?"

"Nothing else," she replied.

"There's a temporal signature in your turbolift," he said, indicating the scanner that Raan had given him. "What do you know of that?"

T'Pol was not sure what a "temporal signature" was but she could make a logical inference based on the name. Once again, she reminded herself of the Vulcan Science Directorate's position on time travel. She was certain that the explanation for the captain's disappearance had to be something more plausible but she had yet to come up with it.

"The last time we saw Captain Archer, he was entering that turbolift," she replied.

Silik thought over the situation for a tense moment. He intentionally drew out the silence, knowing the entire bridge was focused on him. "Perhaps you haven't been lying to me," he said.

The Suliban leader allowed the silence to continue while he formulated his plan. "You," he said, indicating Commander Tucker. "Shut down all com systems and computer terminals with the exception of engineering and the bridge." He then turned to Raan. "Confine all of them to their quarters. If anyone resists . . ." he left the end of his sentence open to the commander's interpretation.

"Understood," Raan said with the slightest hint of a smile.

Raan nodded to a guard who raised his disruptor to Trip and gave the commander a jab in the ribs to emphasize his point.

"Hey!" Trip exclaimed, shooting the guard a withering look.

The Suliban guard answered back with another poke to the midsection.

T'Pol looked at Trip. "Under the circumstances," she said, "it would be best to do what he says, Commander."

Trip considered her words and reluctantly moved to a console to start implementing Silik's orders. His mind was working on how to send a different message out by way of their communications satellite but the guard was watching his every move. He was going to have to do as ordered, for now at least.

Silik nodded to a pair of guards who took the helm and tactical stations. "Plot a course to the Helix," he commanded. "It's time to make a report."

The helmsman programmed the information. Moments later *Enterprise* and its company of cell-ships made a slow turn, reversing direction and heading off at high impulse.

The tense silence that filled the *Enterprise* bridge as it cut its way through space was in stark contrast to the heated discussion taking place light-years away concerning the ship's location. At Starfleet Headquarters, Admiral Forrest was still focused on the headache that was now a few days old. It was the only thing keeping him from pointing out that Ambassador Soval was coming dangerously close to expressing emotion.

"They're three days overdue," the ambassador repeated information that was already well known by the occupants of Forrest's office. A pair of Vulcan dignitaries and Commander Williams rounded out the members of the meeting.

Forrest shot a look at Williams. They both knew this meeting was not going to solve any of their problems. "I told you, Ambassador," the admiral persisted. "Archer said he was returning with proof that they weren't responsible for the tragedy at the Paraagan colony."

Soval leaned back in the guest chair. "You also told me that Starfleet had ordered him to deliver Sub-Commander

T'Pol and his medical officer to the Vulcan ship, *D'kyr,*" the ambassador reminded him. "They're three days overdue."

"The *D'kyr* has long range sensors," Williams interjected, trying to move the conversation forward. "Have they detected *Enterprise?*"

Soval's impatience bordered on anger. "Captain Archer's negligence caused the death of over three thousand colonists," the ambassador persisted. "Your superiors instructed them to return to Earth. Their mission is over. They haven't followed those instructions."

Now Forrest was getting angry. He concentrated on the shooting pain in his head rather than the one sitting in front of him. "You didn't answer the commander's question," he said. "Has your ship detected *Enterprise?*"

Soval took a moment to consider the question. Forrest was quite familiar with the ambassador's pauses. They generally meant that the Vulcans had more information than they were letting on. The moment was solely for Soval to decide whether or not he was going to share what he knew. More often than not, the pause ended with more silence.

"The *D'kyr* said they were joined by a number of other vessels," Soval finally relented in saying. "They're no longer within sensor range."

"What kind of vessels?" Williams asked.

Forrest wanted to know as well. This was a key piece of information. *Enterprise* had made contact with a variety of races since leaving Earth, but Forrest knew of no people with "a number of vessels" who would render aid in this situation. He could only assume that they were in trouble.

"They were at too great a distance to identify," Soval said, abruptly dismissing the important fact. *"Enterprise* has ignored our hails and defied Starfleet's orders. I have no choice but to send the *D'kyr* in pursuit."

"Jonathan Archer doesn't report to you," Forrest said.

"No he doesn't," Soval acknowledged as he stood with his aides flanking him. "But Sub-Commander T'Pol does. And since she would never comply with his present actions, I have to conclude that she is being held against her will."

And they say that we *are guided by unreasonable emotions,* Forrest thought, but chose not to say. There were some lines that shouldn't be crossed at the moment.

Commander Williams spoke instead, saving the admiral from taking the argument to the next level. "I know you don't think much of Archer, Ambassador, but he's not in the habit of kidnapping Vulcans."

Forrest knew that Soval's suggestion was ludicrous, but it did add one more difficult component to the equation. *Is it possible that* Enterprise *may need assistance?* he thought. *We may need the Vulcans to get involved no matter what they may expect from the outcome.*

"Fine, send your ship," Forrest told the ambassador as he played the odds of adding to the conflict against the possibility that *Enterprise* needed reinforcements. "Whatever Archer's up to, I'm sure he's got a good reason. He knows what he's doing."

"Does he, really?" Soval made one last cutting comment before leaving the office with his aides.

"Can you believe that?" Forrest nearly shouted once the

door was closed again. "If we're not murderers, then we must be kidnappers at the very least. What the hell do these people *really* think of us?" It was as if Forrest were releasing all the anger he had been holding in since his first meeting with the Vulcans so many years ago.

"They're just concerned about the sub-commander," Williams offered, hoping to calm his friend. He had never seen the admiral so upset before.

"Don't you dare play devil's advocate with me!" Forrest yelled. "Concern. Worry. Those are emotions. And we know how evil emotions are." It was the first time he had ever voiced his own emotions about the Vulcans in front of another member of Starfleet. He knew it was inappropriate but he also knew that Williams was the one person to whom he could say these things without it coming back to haunt him at some later time.

"Now you and I both know the Vulcans make more of a show out of this whole emotional suppression than they actually practice it," Williams noted with a smile. "Soval's just strutting because he can. It's never bothered you this much before."

"It's never been this serious before," Forrest quietly reminded his friend.

Chapter 15

The massive Suliban Helix hid within the swirling red nebula. It was comprised of hundreds of cell-ships and one lone Starfleet vessel. *Enterprise* was attached at a docking port, tethered to the monstrosity as a prisoner.

Once the ship had docked, and Silik and Raan had confirmed that the crew was locked down, they took the information they had gathered to the temporal chamber. They didn't have Archer, but they had every other member of his crew, his ship, and their recovered data discs. Silik believed that his mysterious benefactor would be satisfied with those successes, if only they could reach him.

"Have you cycled through the sub-temporal harmonics?" Raan asked as he watched Silik anxiously work the controls to the room.

They had been trying to establish contact for several minutes, but the shadowed figure would not answer. The conditions that normally allowed occupants of the room to bridge different time periods refused to initialze. The platform where their benefactor had stood on previous occasions was empty.

Silik hit the sequence of commands one more time hoping it would work, suspecting it was useless. He knew their problem was not a technological one, at least it wasn't on this end of the communiqué. "He's never failed to respond before."

"Perhaps he's angry that we didn't return with Archer," Raan suggested, sounding a little too happy with the idea.

"Archer was not on *Enterprise*," Silik insisted without looking up. He wasn't saying it for Raan's benefit since the commander was well aware of the fact. Silik had hoped that the being from the future could hear him and understand why they had failed in their mission. "Why isn't he responding? I need instructions!"

Raan moved in. He liked seeing Silik in this state. It made his job so much easier. "He said to destroy *Enterprise* if we couldn't bring him Archer. We should tow them out of the nebula and do it now."

"That temporal signature changes everything," Silik said with panic rising in his voice. "If Archer was pulled through time, we need new instructions." He continued to desperately work the console. "Where is he?"

"If he's angry with you," Raan said, enjoying his role as second in command, "you'll be punished again." The commander wasn't exactly upset by the proposition. He assumed that Silik only had a few more failures in him before the role of Cabal leader was reassigned. Being next in command, Raan was more than ready to take over the lead in this faction of the Cold War. Their benefactor was generous with his gifts to the Suliban, but even more so toward the one in charge.

Silik looked to him with eyes ablaze. He knew exactly what Raan had been thinking. It was the same type of thought he would have had if he were in the commander's place.

"We should destroy *Enterprise!*" Raan asserted once again, twisting the knife.

Silik stopped working the console. No answer was going to come. The thought of ridding themselves of the *Enterprise* was tempting, but he knew it would not serve his purpose in the long run. Silik would need more concrete information if he was going to be rewarded once he managed to make contact.

"Have the surgeons prepare," he ordered a disappointed Raan. "Then bring me the Vulcan."

While Silik continued to worry over what was happening in the future, Daniels and Archer were busily trying to figure out what had happened to the past. The pair had taken up a spot on the library floor in the history section. They sat between two high stacks of books, pouring through the piles of reading material that lay around them, quietly working through the dusty collection. Some of the books were so old that the pages crumbled at their touch.

"I haven't found a single reference to this 'Federation'

you talked about," Archer said, ready to give up the search and move onto more pressing concerns.

"I doubt you will," Daniels replied with regret.

"Because the monument wasn't there?"

"Because *you* weren't there," Daniels clarified.

Archer regarded the man skeptically. "So I disappear one day and all history changes?"

Daniels kept reading, trying to maintain the balance between how much information he shared and what he kept to himself. "I've looked through the twenty-first and twenty-second centuries," Daniels finally replied as he skimmed the pages. "Everything looks right up until the warp-five program. After that, *nothing* looks right."

"There were a lot of people involved with the warp-five program," Archer suggested. He thought of the hundreds of people that had contributed to the project, including his own father.

"We didn't bring 'a lot of people' here this morning," Daniels corrected him. "We just brought you."

Archer took a deep breath. The reality of the situation was finally sinking in. Earth—however it was defined— was no more. If all that Daniels was saying had been true, humanity had ceased to exist. Whether it had ended in one violent moment or slowly over time really didn't matter to Archer. He found both concepts equally terrifying, especially considering that it was all because of him.

He pushed past his thoughts. They would only lead him down a path that he was not ready to pursue. He picked up another book, reading its title off the spine. " *'The Romulan Star Empire'*? What's that?"

"Maybe you shouldn't be reading that book," Daniels suggested, taking it out of the captain's hands and offering one on the subject of the Denobulans. That was a race with which Archer was considerably more familiar. Knowing more about them shouldn't affect history once they finally set things right.

"I don't get it," Archer said, ignoring the book. His mind returned to thoughts about himself. "What could I have done that could've been so important?"

"It wasn't just you," Daniels clarified. "It was events you helped set in motion."

"This timeline," Archer pressed on. "The one you say doesn't exist. What can you tell me about it? If my mission had continued?"

Daniels put down the book on Romulans so he could focus on the question.

"It would have led to others," Daniels said, choosing his words very carefully.

"And?"

But Daniels knew that was just about all he could reveal on that particular subject. He stared blankly at Archer, silently pleading with the man to accept the fact that there were just some things that could not be told.

"Okay, what about this Federation?" Archer tried a new angle. "Was Earth part of it? Was I part of it?"

Daniels stood among the piles of books. Maybe he had to stop worrying about the long lost history and focus on the events that had led them to this horrific present. His mind was working to piece together the dilemma before him by using whatever information he had on hand.

"Silik wanted you," Daniels said, "not the data discs. The people he answered to were more interested in capturing Jonathan Archer than in blaming *Enterprise* for the destruction of the colony. They obviously knew what role you were going to play in the months or years to come." Daniels laughed at the very irony of the situation. "By taking you away from the twenty-second century I caused exactly what I was trying to prevent."

Who was aware of what I would do? Archer thought. *Why do they want to destroy this Federation? How did they know my abduction would cause its end?* Dozens more questions rushed to the captain's mind. He tried to factor through what Daniels had said, but the concepts were beginning to overwhelm him. "You've lost me."

"The only chance I have of restoring my century is by getting you back to yours," he replied simply, although he knew the challenges involved in making the idea into reality.

"Sounds like you've got a 'chicken and the egg' problem," Archer noted.

Now it was Daniels's turn to look lost, puzzled by what the man had said.

Obviously some colloquialisms did not survive history, Archer thought. He wasn't sure if that was a good or bad thing.

Archer clarified his comment. "You said all your time portals were gone—and your technology. There isn't even electricity here. You going to find a bicycle and turn it into a time machine?"

Daniels thought over the captain's comment. He knew Archer was just being facetious, but there was a glimmer of an idea behind the comment. His mind focused on the idea of going back to basics. "Maybe we don't need a time machine," he said. "Do you have your communicator?"

"And a scanner," Archer replied as he removed the items from his uniform pockets.

"May I?" he asked, taking the technology from the captain. "The people the Suliban were working for came from three hundred years ago. They couldn't travel through time, but they did develop a way to send back images of themselves to communicate through time."

"You can't do that with those," Archer said, nodding to the devices.

"No, it's a little more complicated," Daniels said as he looked over the items, "but not much. We learned how to do it in high school. But we're going to need a few things that might not be too easy to find."

Archer was pleased to hear that they finally had the beginning of a plan. It didn't matter that he wasn't sure what Daniels was suggesting. He was ready to do anything.

"What are we waiting for?" he asked as they moved out from the stacks.

Chapter 16

Mayweather lay in his bed with his uniform jacket open. He stared at the wall feeling entirely useless. His place was at the helm, guiding the ship and its crew into the unknown. There was very little for a helmsman to do while trapped in his quarters. His mind worked on a way to escape, but he was just one man against an army of Suliban. He could hardly mount an effective offensive alone.

The irony of the situation was not lost on him, however. He was being held by the same race of people he had recently helped escape from a prison camp. Sure, the Suliban he had worked with at the Tandaran detention complex did not share the motives of his captors, but they all came from the same place of origin. They had shared a homeworld centuries ago. They lived the same nomadic lifestyle. They looked pretty much the same—most of the time. But it was more than just genetic enhancements that made them different.

JANUARY 2152
Two Months Ago

Mayweather woke on a thin floor mat in an unfurnished, dilapidated cell lit solely by a shaft of sunlight that streamed in through a barred window. He was not alone. Captain Archer was lying on a mat beside him, unconscious. The ensign unsuccessfully tried to wake his captain but Archer would not rise. Concerned, Mayweather got to his feet, intending to search for help and, with hope, figure out where they were.

He tried the door to their cell and was surprised to find that it opened easily into a hall. Several additional cell doors lined the corridor. He looked past them in search of life wondering where they had been taken and what they had done to cause their imprisonment. The last thing he remembered was coming under fire when he and the captain had taken their shuttlepod to explore some energy readings behind an alien moon.

The sound of footsteps approaching kept Mayweather from actually stepping out of his cell. He ducked back inside leaving the door open a crack to watch as the shadowy figures of two humanoid men approached. When the figures drew closer, he could make out the dappled texture of their skin. He had never seen these aliens firsthand before, but he knew from description what he was looking at—Suliban.

Mayweather stealthily followed the men through the complex. They led him to a large common room where additional members of their race had gathered. Mayweather stuck to the shadows as he took in the frightening sight. Suliban filled the complex. He returned to the cell and reported on the dire situation.

Archer took in what Mayweather had told him. The best way to proceed was by gathering as much information as they could. Since their captors had seen fit to allow them to leave their cell, the captain assumed it would be rude not to accept the little freedom they had been granted. Mayweather led him back to the communal room where they happened across a Suliban woman carrying a metal container filled with water. The woman stopped upon seeing them.

"You're the new arrivals," she noted in a flat tone. Her voice did not betray how she felt about their arrival in the facility.

"Why are we here?" Archer asked, assuming that she was one of the Suliban holding them prisoner.

"Why are any of us here?" she replied with an edge.

Mayweather and Archer exchanged a puzzled look. Before the captain could ask another question, a Klaxon sounded throughout the complex. The woman immediately put down her water as cell doors along the hall swung open and more Suliban came pouring out. They all joined the woman in rows as they seemed to line up for inspection. The *Enterprise* officers stood where they were, unsure of what to do.

The pair watched as a small team of guards entered through a wall hatch. Mayweather did not recognize their race, but he immediately noticed how closely they resembled humans. He briefly wondered if they were Suliban disguised in their chameleon mode. *But why would they be in disguise among their own?* he quickly realized the flaw in his thinking.

One of the Suliban standing at attention dropped the small cup he was holding. When he bent to pick it up, the lead guard jabbed the man with some kind of stun stick, forcing the Suliban to stand straight. The guards continued through the ranks until they reached Archer and Mayweather.

"Follow me," the leader ordered the *Enterprise* officers.

The guard, named Major Klev, led them through the complex where they saw more Suliban standing at attention. They wound their way into the office of Colonel Grat, the military officer in charge of the facility. Grat apologized for not speaking with them sooner and explained they had been brought to the detention complex because their shuttle had stumbled into the Tandaran military zone.

"Does everybody that violates your territory get thrown into a place like this?" Mayweather asked, having never come across this race before.

"We're at war with a species that can mimic the appearance of almost any humanoid," Grat explained without apology. "We had to be certain that you weren't infiltrators."

"If you're worried we're Suliban," the ensign replied, "trust me, we're not."

"I know. We've already tested your DNA," he said in a dismissive tone before turning his attention to Archer. "You're familiar with the Cabal?"

"Unfortunately," Archer replied, taking a seat across from the colonel.

"Then you must know about their genetic enhancements," Grat noted. "And how dangerous they can be."

"Firsthand," Archer replied, deciding to play things close to the vest until he could be sure of what was going on.

"I hope you haven't suffered too many casualties," Grat replied.

"We've been lucky so far," the captain answered.

Grat went on to explain that he could not release the Starfleet officers until they appeared before a magistrate on Tandar Prime. In the meantime, Archer and Mayweather would be "guests" of the overcrowded detention complex until the planetary transport would arrive in three days. When Archer asked to contact his ship, the request was denied. However, the colonel did assure them he would speak with the *Enterprise*'s crew solely and inform them of the situation to ensure that they did not interfere.

That night, Archer and Mayweather found the "proper meal" they had been promised to be less than satisfactory. Afterward the captain went to the common area for some water. He saw a Suliban man hurrying to remove clothing from a line. The man was putting the hastily rolled clothes into a basket being held by a young girl that Archer assumed to be the man's daughter. The captain started to leave the area, but something held him back. He turned to the man.

"I can't believe you'd do this to a child," Archer said

with barely concealed contempt as he walked over to the laundry line.

"Do what?" the man asked, honestly unaware of what the stranger was talking about.

"She seems a little young to be part of the Cabal." Archer pointed to the girl.

"You don't know what you're talking about."

"I know you're given genetic tricks as payment," Archer said, forgetting about the water. "What are they giving her?"

An alarm sounded.

"I don't know who you are," the Suliban said as he loaded the last of his clothing into the basket in a rush, "but you're wrong about us."

"Is that so?"

"We're not genetically enhanced," he said, "and we're not members of the Cabal."

Archer didn't believe him. "If that's true, then what are you doing here?"

"Didn't Colonel Grat tell you?" the man asked with sarcasm as he tried to make his way out of the room. "We're dangerous. All Suliban are dangerous."

Archer hadn't noticed that during their exchange all the other Suliban had left the area—not until Major Klev entered the nearly deserted room. Klev was not happy to find the Suliban, named Danik, out of his cell. Although Archer tried to accept the blame for delaying the Suliban father, the major refused to listen. He insisted that Danik spend a night in isolation. Danik surprised Archer by quickly agreeing to the punishment, expressing concern only for his daughter's well-being.

During their time at the detention center, Archer and Mayweather saw several examples of Suliban behavior that challenged their original misconceptions. These people did not seem to be involved in any Temporal Cold War. They were just living their lives confined within the walls of the complex. When Archer ran into Danik after the Suliban had been released from isolation, he asked him to explain their situation. At first Danik was reluctant to answer, but eventually he welcomed the two *Enterprise* officers into his cell for a conversation.

"We're not criminals, Captain," Danik explained. "And we're not soldiers. The only thing we're guilty of is being Suliban."

Archer couldn't understand why they were being held. "They must have tested your DNA and figured out that you haven't been genetically altered."

Danik nearly laughed at the absurd comment. "As far as they're concerned that doesn't mean anything." His mood turned even more serious. "You believed I was a member of the Cabal, didn't you?"

Archer was reluctant to admit the truth.

"Didn't you?" Danik pressed.

"Yes, I did," Archer said.

"All that seems to matter is the way we look," he said.

Archer was stung by the comment that he could not argue.

" 'Be careful of their wicked smiles,' " Danik recited,

" 'their shining yellow eyes. At night they'll squeeze right through your door and everybody dies.' " He turned back to the men. "Tandaran children used to tease my daughter with that nursery rhyme. At least here she doesn't have to hear it anymore." The bitterness in his voice betrayed the lighthearted comment.

"This is an internment camp," Archer said, realizing the truth behind the detention center.

"Detention Complex Twenty-six," Danik sarcastically corrected him. "I've heard it's one of their nicer ones."

"Why did this happen?"

"The Cabal began their attacks eight years ago," Danik explained. "It wasn't long before the Tandarans started to question the loyalty of all Suliban living in their territory. We were rounded up—'relocated' as they like to say. They told us it would only be temporary. It was for our own safety. 'Once the Cabal has been destroyed you'll be free to go back to your home,' " he added in a mocking tone with his anger growing. "We're still waiting."

Danik took a moment to attempt to reign in his emotions, but failed. "There are eighty-nine people here," he continued, "thousands more in the other camps. Every one of us used to be citizens of the worlds in the Tandar Sector. Did you know I was born in the same town as one of the guards? Major Klev. I was friends with his brother while I was growing up."

"What about the government on the Suliban homeworld?" Mayweather chimed in with the question. "Don't they have something to say about this?"

"I'm sure they would if they existed," Danik replied. "Our homeworld became uninhabitable three hundred years ago. Most Suliban are nomadic. But, some of us have assimilated into other cultures. My grandfather made the unfortunate decision to settle on Tandar Prime."

Their conversation was interrupted when another Suliban, one named Sajen, entered the cell. This man was far less welcoming to the humans than Danik had been. He brought with him the regretful news that Danik's wife had been denied yet another request to be transferred to their facility. The couple had been trying to get back together ever since they were separated during the relocation.

As the *Enterprise* officers continued to bond with the Suliban detainees, Archer was called to Colonel Grat's office once again. After berating the captain for his altercation with Danik the previous night, the colonel moved on to the real reason he had called Archer to his office. Grat had learned from the Tandaran intelligence agency all about the *Enterprise* crew's earlier dealings with the Suliban Cabal and he wanted to know more about it. He questioned the captain, but now Archer refused to answer anything. Their conversation quickly grew heated.

"What exactly do you want?" Archer asked, growing impatient with the line of questioning.

"Information," Grat replied. "What do you know about the Cabal? What kind of genetic enhancements have you seen? Helix deployments? Who's giving them their orders?"

"You've got plenty of Suliban here," Archer said, testing the colonel. "Why not ask them?"

Grat paused for a beat, realizing that Archer fully understood the situation. "We both know that they wouldn't be very helpful."

His suspicions had been confirmed. "Then why are they in prison?"

"That's a discussion for another time," Grat replied with a dismissive tone.

"There are families down there," Archer noted with his temper rising. "One man hasn't seen his wife in years."

Grat ignored him. "Tell me what you know!"

"They don't deserve this kind of treatment!"

"They're here for their own protection," Grat replied, his words smacking of political rhetoric.

"Oh, really?" Archer said, sarcastically.

The colonel took a moment to compose himself. "The last thing we wanted to do was build these detention centers," he explained, trying to sound genuine. "But we had no choice. When the Cabal began their activities there was a great deal of fear among the Tandarans. There were incidents of violence." His voice rose in passion. "Fourteen innocent Suliban were killed in one day alone. We had to find a way to keep them out of danger."

"Why not just let them find another place to live?"

"They wouldn't get very far," Grat said with intensity. "It's ironic, but once they were out of Tandaran territory, the Cabal would hunt them all down and turn them into soldiers. They're better off here."

"I've met a few Suliban who would disagree," Archer challenged his comment.

Grat steered the subject back to his inquisition, asking about the incident in which Silik had infiltrated *Enterprise* to stop the warp core breach. When Archer refused to answer, the colonel suggested that he could keep the *Enterprise* officers from making it to their transport to Tandar Prime and remaining a guest of the detention center for the foreseeable future. He gave Archer time to think about his decision.

In the days that followed, Grat again made contact with *Enterprise*, informing the crew that there was a delay in the proceedings, but failing to provide them with the actual reason. This time the crew was able to lock onto Grat's signal and trace it back to the source. T'Pol had them set a course to rescue their crewmates.

In the meantime Archer grew closer with the Suliban detainees while learning the details of a past escape attempt that had gone awry. He noted that *Enterprise* should be coming after them soon and set to work on his own plans for escape.

Meanwhile Mayweather tried to befriend the angry Sajen.

"Writing a letter?" Mayweather asked as he sat beside Sajen on a bench in the common area.

The Suliban continued writing in his native language, barely glancing up at Mayweather. "It's a journal," he replied sharply.

"Could be valuable one day," Mayweather commented,

undeterred by the attitude he was receiving. "People will want to know what happened here."

"I doubt anyone will ever read this," Sajen replied cynically.

"Then why are you writing it?"

"Why do you care?" Sajen shot back.

Mayweather was taken aback by the intensity of the response and chose not to answer him.

Sajen leaned forward, adopting a confrontational attitude. "I see how you look at us," he spat. "You wouldn't be surprised if I slithered up this wall or turned my face inside out." His anger was overwhelming them both. "Cabal. Suliban. It's all the same to you."

"That's not true," Mayweather replied, wishing there was some way to convince the man.

Sajen replied with a skeptical glare before storming off.

Mayweather remained at the table. He was deeply troubled by the encounter.

That night as Mayweather slept, *Enterprise* arrived in orbit and the crew managed to beam down a communicator to the captain. Once in contact he refused their offer of rescue, informing T'Pol that he was going to help the Suliban escape. Though the Vulcan was skeptical of his plan to interfere with the alien culture, she agreed to help.

The next morning Archer shared the plan with Danik. The Suliban was similarly doubtful of their chances, but he agreed to do as the captain said. Sajen, however, balked at the risk in trusting these humans whom they had just met. Danik ignored his friend and went about to convince the other detainees. But Grat had come across evidence of Archer's communication with his ship. He called the captain to his office.

Archer refused to answer Grat's questions, even when the colonel presented a beaten Mayweather to the captain. Grat had found the communicator on the ensign, but Mayweather had refused to reveal anything about the device. When Archer continued to remain silent, he was placed in isolation as punishment.

The *Enterprise* crew crafted an escape plan. Reed would accept the risk of beaming down to the planet in a Suliban disguise, Trip would cover the escape from above in a shuttlepod. As the plans progressed, Grat used the captured communicator to contact the ship, letting him know that he was on to them. T'Pol refused to be cowed and continued working on the escape.

Mayweather splashed water on his bruised face while waiting for some kind of signal from the ship. He hadn't seen the captain since he was led away to isolation.

"What happened to you?" Sajen asked as he came up behind the beaten ensign.

"What do you care?" he threw the Suliban's own words back at him with an edge.

Sajen decided to ignore the challenge. "Danik's been looking for your captain. Have you seen him?"

"You might try isolation," Mayweather replied, finally

turning to face the Suliban. "Still think we're working for the Tandarans?"

Sajen answered by way of his silence.

Mayweather's temper flared at the ungrateful alien. "You know, we could've left this place a long time ago if Captain Archer hadn't decided to help you."

"I never asked for your help."

"Why? Because we're not Suliban? Because we look a little too much like Tandarans?" Mayweather suspected that he had hit a nerve with that one. "I'll admit, when I first came here it wasn't easy to see past my preconceptions about the Suliban. But I did. Why can't you?"

He stormed off without waiting for a response.

Once everything was in place, T'Pol managed to jam the Tandaran sensors and launch the rescue mission. Reed was beamed down in Suliban guise. With Danik's help, the lieutenant freed the captain and set charges throughout the complex. As *Enterprise* fought off a Tandaran attack, Trip launched a shuttlepod and headed for the facility.

As the buildings of the detention complex came under fire from outside and within, Archer led the Suliban to the docking bay and their captured ships. Sajen had learned to trust the humans and risked his own life to save his friend Danik. The *Enterprise* crew watched from their shuttlepod as Suliban ships lifted off the planet heading for whatever new home they could find.

Mayweather considered all that they had witnessed in the past few days as the shuttlepod rose up to meet *Enter-*

prise. The enemy that he had originally been prepared to hate without question had surprised him by not being an adversary at all. He suspected that it would make future dealings with the Suliban more difficult. It was easy to fight against an evil opponent, but he now knew there were several sides to this story and many facets to this alien race. He worried for his new friends as their ships moved off into the distance.

"Do you think they'll make it, sir?" he quietly asked his captain.

"Do I think they'll get out of Tandaran space safely?" Archer replied, thoughtfully. "Yes. Do I think they'll be all right?"

The captain let the statement hang in the air, unanswered.

Chapter 17

Silik couldn't help but appreciate the situation he had created. The Vulcan Sub-Commander was restrained in the same surgical chair he had sat in when given his genetic enhancing gifts. It was the same chair he had been in when some of those gifts were stripped away as well. But now, he was the one in power. Silik was going to get his answers no matter what he had to do to the Vulcan in the process.

He looked over at the surgeons who were monitoring the machine that was connected to the woman's body. Several tubes were attached to her body administering a clear liquid into her bloodstream. The surgeons indicated that it was all right for Silik to proceed. The drugs were beginning to take effect.

"Where is Archer?" he asked, hovering over T'Pol.

"I don't know."

Silik didn't like that answer. "Who are you working with from the future?"

"The Vulcan Science Directorate has determined that time travel is impossible," she stated concisely and honestly.

Silik wondered if she was playing games with him, but suspected it was not in the nature of her race to do so. He looked back to the surgeons who silently confirmed that the drugs should be working. "Does Captain Archer agree with that opinion?"

"It is not an opinion."

Silik's body tensed. Part of him was tempted to make her watch as he destroyed her ship, but he knew that would not give him the ultimate satisfaction he required. His benefactor wanted answers, not senseless destruction. Their plans were more calculated than that. Every move they made had a specific purpose. Even without contact from the future, Silik was determined to continue behaving in the manner he had been trained.

He continued the interrogation by carefully rephrasing the question. "Does Captain Archer agree with that *determination*."

"Captain Archer believes that Crewman Daniels comes from the future."

Silik latched onto the fact that she had referred to the time traveler in the present tense. "But Daniels is dead."

"Captain Archer claims he saw Daniels two days ago."

A smile crept over the Suliban's face. "Your captain is gone," he continued. "Did Daniels take him into the past or the future?"

"The Vulcan Science Directorate has determined that time travel is impossible."

The smile slipped away.

Archer stumbled down the stairwell, holding fast to the railing. He was back in the building where he had first arrived in the thirty-first century. Daniels was busy working on his plan and had sent the captain in search of additional equipment. His current mission was to find some copper. It wasn't quite as exciting as leading a starship into the unknown, but Archer already had enough excitement that morning to last several lifetimes.

The copper hunt turned up nothing on the floor where Daniels had been working in what Archer assumed to be the man's former apartment. Apparently advancements had been made in the field of construction in the time between Archer's disappearance and humanity's destruction. The copper that was often used in the piping and wiring of buildings in the twenty-second century had been replaced by some amalgam of metals that Daniels had explained was much easier to work with. It would be very hard to find a pure sample of copper in a residential area. One would think a search for copper would be easy enough in a building with its innards exposed, but Archer was begining to realize that this particular search could take a while.

The typical conundrum of the inventor, Archer thought. *We keep looking for new and different when old and ordinary worked just fine.*

The door crashed back into the stairwell as Archer

stepped into the hallway of a lower floor in the building. He moved to the open apartment across from the stairwell and stepped inside. It looked like a family had once lived there. What appeared to be a child's playpen had been shoved against a wall. A mobile hung from a bar stretched across the top. Little plastic dolphins and whales dangled on several wires. Archer gave it a little push and watched the sea mammals spin. He wondered if any animals had survived the future and naturally thought back to his own companion.

I wonder if I'll ever see Porthos again. Or anyone I ever knew. What will happen to my crew if I never get home? Will Hoshi give up on space exploration for good? Does Trip really understand how important his friendship has been to me? What will happen to T'Pol when she goes back to Vulcan? Will she forget all that she's learned about humanity?

Archer turned away from the playpen, briefly regretting the fact that he had not had time for children of his own. This was a thought he didn't often allow himself to express. He had long since made peace with the fact that his career would not allow for long-lasting romantic entanglements. However, considering the situation he was in, he couldn't help but think about it as he moved through the living area in search of copper.

What if Daniels's plan doesn't work and I'm stuck here forever? Will Daniels be the only other person I see for the rest of my life? The only person I speak to? The only person who exists?

A thorough search of the living area and sleeping quarters showed no sign of the metal. He moved into the kitchen, figuring that that would be the most likely place to find what he was looking for. Curiosity drew him to what he assumed to be the food storage area. He braced himself for whatever foul items could be inside. Archer had no alternative; he needed to know. A quick look—and a quick smell—confirmed his suspicions. Whatever had happened on the planet had occurred before the residents had a chance to empty their refrigerator. Archer closed the door, but the stench lingered for a few minutes.

What will I do?

The apartment search proved fruitless and Archer stepped back into the hall. He looked left and right and noted that there were roughly the same number of doorways on either side. Some had doors still hanging in the frames while others were entirely open to the world. He moved to the right, continuing his search.

Daniels had set to work on a device that might help them restore the timeline. He stood in the midst of the ancient rubble that according to his memory had looked quite different mere hours ago. He had carefully removed the guts of Archer's equipment and spread it out on a ramshackle table along with some other components that had been collected. The grime clung to his sweaty body as he worked over the devices, repositioning circuits and delicate components with the makeshift tools.

A short time later Archer entered through what was left of the doorway. He was carrying a wooden ladle with an intricately decorated handle wrapped in a substance that had the brownish-green patina of tarnished copper. It appeared that his search had apparently been successful, but at a price. He was just as much a mess as Daniels.

"I can't be sure, but I think this is copper," Archer said as he handed the ladle over.

Daniels touched the handle to his tongue, testing the material. "Well done." He kept working as he dictated his instructions. "I need you to unwrap it and pound it into small strips no more that a millimeter thick."

Archer scanned the room for a tool. He picked up a piece of concrete that had once been part of the wall. Its edges were jagged and hard to hold without digging into the skin, but Archer knew it was the best thing available. He held the sharp end of the piece against the end of the ladle and set to work pounding down the copper.

On the captive *Enterprise*, Reed was pacing his quarters, restlessly. The small cabin felt like it was shrinking, closing in with each step. As *Enterprise*'s tactical officer, he bore the full weight of responsibility for the overrun ship even though there had been nothing that he could have done to stop it. Reed was not handling the inaction well. He needed to get out. He needed to retake the ship.

His mind was so filled with frustrated thoughts that at first he didn't hear the static sound piercing the silence of his cabin. Once he realized that the sound was not in his imagination he wondered if some piece of equipment was malfunctioning, perhaps the lights or environmental controls. But it slowly became evident that the noise was not just some arbitrary sound; it was repeating in some kind of pattern.

Reed stopped his pacing and listened. He was able to trace the static to the small panel beside the door. Leaning his ear closer to the panel he thought he could make out something buried in the static. A voice. Someone was trying to communicate with him.

"Hello?" he said tentatively into the panel.

A burst of static came back at him, carrying with it an unintelligible voice. He couldn't even be sure if it was male or female.

"Please repeat," he said, clearly annunciating each word. "I can't understand."

The static changed, but the voice remained incoherent.

"I still can't hear you," Reed said. "Try modulating the sub-carrier wave."

"Malcolm, it's me—Trip." The commander's voice fritzed in and out as he spoke. "Can you hear me?"

"Barely," Reed replied. "You're going to need to boost the signal."

Reed waited for the adjustment.

"Any better?" Trip asked, his voice coming through considerably more clearly.

"Yes, I thought the com was offline," Reed said.

"It is," Trip replied from his quarters. "I'm routing the

signal through the EPS grid. I can talk to any doorbell on B-deck."

Trip was standing by his own door using a thin instrument to tweak a jumble of circuitry hanging out of the small open panel he was speaking into. The circuitry had been jury-rigged and reconfigured to work in a way it was not originally intended.

"Are you all right?" Reed's slightly staticy voice came through the panel.

"Same as you, I guess," Trip replied as he looked around his cramped quarters. The Helix could be seen out his port. "Locked in tight."

"How about the others?"

"I can't get in contact with T'Pol for some reason," Trip said, trying not to worry again about why the sub-commander had not replied when he had made contact with her doorbell. "Hoshi and Travis are on C-deck."

"Any thoughts about how we're going to get rid of these Suliban?" Reed asked with anticipation.

"One step at a time," Trip replied. "First thing I need to do is figure out how to tap into the door-coms on C-deck. I'll get back to you. Sit tight."

"I wasn't planning on going anywhere," Reed replied.

Chapter 18

Admiral Forrest turned down the lights in his office, relishing the first moment of silence he'd had since receiving Archer's news about the Paraagan Colony. His headache persisted. It had gone away for a brief period after Archer told him the evidence to clear *Enterprise*. Then it returned with a vengeance around the time the Vulcans informed him that Archer and his crew had inexplicably cut off communication.

Jonathan would never kidnap T'Pol, he thought. The admiral didn't have to convince himself of that. He knew the man well enough. Forrest had also gotten the feeling from Archer's more recent updates that the Vulcan woman had become more integrated into the crew. *But not so much that she would blindly ignore her superiors for days. Something is definitely wrong.*

The door chime sounded. Forrest allowed a moment to

pass before answering. He wasn't ready for his headache to intensify.

"Yes?" he replied.

His aide entered through the open door. He was prudently carrying a steaming cup of something that was obviously intended for the admiral.

"Coffee sir?" he offered. "I was thinking the caffeine could help."

"It certainly couldn't hurt," Forrest replied, relieved over the fact that it wasn't another problem walking in the door. He accepted the coffee with a nod of appreciation.

"Begging the admiral's pardon . . ." the aide started, standing nearly at attention. "But, um, permission to speak freely?"

"Why so formal?" Forrest asked. He knew that he scared the kid at times, but they rarely fell into the clipped type of banter he usually expected from cadets. "Sit down."

"Sir," the aide replied as he took a seat. "I was wondering. We were all wondering. What happens now?"

Forrest knew that the "we" the aide was referring to was not just the admiral's staff. The question was on the lips of everyone in Starfleet.

"Now, you go home," Forrest replied, knowing that wasn't what the kid was asking. "The day's over. There's no schedule for tomorrow because we don't know what's going to hit the fan yet."

"No, sir. I meant . . ."

"I know," Forrest replied, knowing that he could continue to evade that question; he had been doing so all day. He told his aide the truth, "I don't know what's next."

"We don't have any idea where *Enterprise* is?"

"No," the admiral replied. "And we have no way of finding out either. At least not without the help of the Vulcans."

"Doesn't Starfleet have some kind of contingency plan?" he asked. "Some way to get to the crew if there's a problem?"

"This was our first test of the warp-five engine," the admiral said, knowing that his aide already knew that. The kid just wanted reassurances that Forrest couldn't give. "We have no other ships that can go out as far as *Enterprise*. At least not in a timeframe that would do them any good."

"What about civilian ships?" the aide suggested. "Transports? Cargo ships?"

"We've tried contacting everyone we had a record of in that part of space," the admiral said. "Even several alien races. I'm afraid at the moment, we're at the mercy of the Vulcans."

The admiral could tell that his aide wanted to speak freely, but the kid was too well trained.

"It's okay," Forrest said. "It's just you and me. You can say it."

"Well, wasn't it a little premature of us to send *Enterprise* out there totally on its own?" The aide was practically squirming in his seat. Sure, he was just repeating the buzz that had been going around the building, but now he was relaying it to the highest ranking officer around. "I mean, we have no recourse to help in emergencies."

"That's the thing about exploration," Forrest replied.

"The risk is oftentimes as great as the benefits—greater. Think of the early explorers sailing off into the unknown. They were told they could fall off the edge of the Earth, but it didn't stop them. Archer and his crew knew the risks when they accepted the mission. True, they weren't prepared for *all* the danger they would encounter, but they certainly were aware of the fact that they were on their own."

"The Vulcans think . . ."

"Every member of that crew is a hero," Forrest interrupted, not caring to hear about what the Vulcans thought. "I have no doubt they are doing whatever they can to get back in contact with us. I have the utmost faith in Jonathan Archer."

Almost a thousand years in the future, Jonathan Archer was having a difficult time keeping faith in the man he knew only as Daniels. He wasn't even sure if it was the man's real name. Archer watched as the collection of circuitry and scavenged parts began beginning to take the shape at Daniels's hands. He still wasn't exactly sure what they were doing, but he wasn't about to ask for an explanation. Aside from the fact that he already knew Daniels was not exactly generous with information, he suspected that he wouldn't understand much of whatever Daniels was willing to divulge. It would be the equivalent of Archer trying to teach Ben Franklin how to build a medical scanner. Sure, the old guy was intelligent enough, but the amount of technological advancements in the years between them eradicated any chance for a productive discussion.

Instead, Archer busied himself by pounding down another strip of copper with the chunk of concrete. He had already been rather productive and a number of thin strips were laid out in a row in front of him. It still wasn't clear if they would be used as casing for the device or some kind of antenna, but Archer continued pounding away, beating out some of his feelings of frustration over being so helpless.

"Any luck?" Archer asked as he looked over at the partially constructed device.

"I still have the spatial coordinates of *Enterprise*," Daniels replied. "But without a quantum discriminator it's going to be very tricky to contact the ship on the same day you left."

"I thought you built these things in high school," Archer said with a smile, tweaking the man.

"Where quantum discriminators were on every desk," Daniels replied with a light sense of smugness.

Archer took a break from the pounding. "Why is the same day so important?" he asked. "What would be wrong with making contact a week before I left, or a month before?"

Daniels looked up from his work. The expression on his face served as a needless reminder of the seriousness of their situation. "I made the biggest mistake in the history of time travel this morning," he said resolutely. "I don't intend to make it any worse."

The words hung in the fetid air for a moment. Archer pushed past his own emotions to imagine what Daniels had been going through. It was one thing for Archer to realize that this bleak future was the result of his being pulled out of time. It was quite another to have been the person doing the pulling.

The men returned to their work with a renewed sense of diligence.

A pair of armed Suliban soldiers accompanied a semiconscious T'Pol to her quarters. The drugs were still in her system and she was having trouble staying up on her feet. She needed to lean on her captors for support. The haze in her field of vision made it difficult to traverse the halls, but she tried to collect any information she could from the trip. Other Suliban passed them as they made their way through the corridor. Some carried their weapons at the ready while others had them holstered. She wondered just how many soldiers were still on the ship.

T'Pol was unaware of the fact that they had reached her quarters until the door was opened and she was dragged inside. The two soldiers roughly deposited her into a chair. It felt good to sit without being restrained. She hadn't realized how much she had been straining the muscles in her legs to simply walk.

The Suliban left the room without comment. Content to see them go, T'Pol remained slumped in her chair, shivering slightly. She tried using a meditation technique to focus her drug-clouded mind, but could not remember how to begin the procedure.

After a brief rest T'Pol pulled herself back up to her feet. Her body was still shaking and it ached to stand. She tried not to stumble as she carried herself into the bathroom, activating the lights as she entered. Her eyes refocused on the room as she stepped over to the sink and tapped the controls.

She leaned forward, hoping to splash some water on her face, but her hands were shaking so badly that she couldn't manage to cup them to hold the liquid. The water just poured through her fingers and disappeared into the drain. The motion of the flowing water nearly hypnotized her.

Eventually T'Pol gave up on the fruitless endeavor and turned off the spout. She pushed her way back into the room, noticing the Helix outside the port for the first time. *That was where they took me,* she remembered.

She wanted to go over to the port to see just how dire the crew's situation was, but her legs could not carry her any farther. T'Pol collapsed onto her bunk. The withdrawal from the truth serum hit her hard as she lay there, trembling.

An odd modulating sound rang through her ears. She assumed it was another side effect of the drugs that had been pumped through her system and tried to ignore it, but the sound refused to go away. As her mind began to clear, T'Pol realized the sound was not in her head. She turned an ear away from her pillow, trying to discern the direction from which the sound was emanating. It was above her.

T'Pol squinted her eyes to focus on a pulsing yellow light that had appeared on the overhead. She watched in a daze as the light gradually took on the shape of a humanoid face, staring down at her, although she could not make out the features. The modulating sound slowed into a rhythmic pattern. Someone was speaking to her. The flickering image on the ceiling continued to sharpen. It was beginning to look familiar to her. The voice, she remembered, was that of a friend.

Jonathan Archer's face hovered above her, his visage heavily distorted and almost spinning. The voice was barely understandable as he spoke. ". . . Captain Archer. Can you hear me? T'Pol this is Captain Archer. Can you hear me?"

T'Pol stared at the strange, swirling image. Her mind was clear enough to worry about the fact that she was hallucinating. The concerns that she had for the captain's safety had obviously manifested into the vision above her.

"T'Pol, this is Captain Archer. Can you hear me?" the image asked again.

Archer's image seemed to turned away from her.

Where are you going? she thought.

"I don't think it's working," he said to some unseen person.

T'Pol looked for someone else in the room, but it was just her and the floating head. She waited for the other person to respond, but heard nothing. Suddenly the image in front of her began to sharpen.

Archer turned back to her. "T'Pol this is Captain Archer. Can you hear me?"

"I don't know where he is," she responded, thinking this was another of Silik's tricks.

"You don't know where who is?" Archer's face asked back.

T'Pol remained silent.

"Sub-Commander, this is Captain Archer," he persisted. "I'm having trouble understanding you."

"Captain Archer's gone," T'Pol insisted through her daze. "A temporal reading in the turbolift. I don't know where he is."

"Daniels brought me to the future," he explained. "That's what the temporal reading was about."

She continued to stare at his image, focusing on Archer's increasingly familiar features as she tried to orient herself to what was occurring. The haze slowly began to lift.

"Are you all right?" Archer asked.

"The Science Vulcan Directorate has determined that time travel is . . . not fair."

The haze had only lifted so far.

"Whatever you say," Archer tried to move their conversation to more logical topics. "Just tell me—are you all right?"

"We're all confined to our quarters."

"Where are you?"

"I told you," she insisted, "in my quarters."

"No, I mean *Enterprise,*" he said. "Where's *Enterprise?*"

She groggily turned her head to the side. "There's a Helix out my port."

"Listen to me, T'Pol," Archer said firmly, hoping that she could focus on his voice. "I need your help. You're going to have to find a way to get to Daniels's quarters. Do you understand me?"

"You're on the ceiling," T'Pol said as if she was realizing that fact for the first time. "Why aren't you on a monitor?"

"There's no technology where I am," he said.

"I thought you said you were in the future," she said, growing more confused.

"T'Pol do you remember when I asked you to keep an open mind?" he asked.

She searched her memory. The words were finally starting to make sense. "Yes."

"There's a lot more at stake here than bringing me back, or the mission," he insisted. "I need you to listen to me very carefully. I need you to trust me."

T'Pol pushed the last of the clouds from her mind as she sat up in bed, ready to hear the captain's plan.

Chapter 19

Mayweather couldn't help but think of telephone party lines of the early-twentieth century, or more accurately the intricate web of conference calls that had evolved decades later. Commander Tucker had managed yet another engineering marvel hooking up communication between the doorbells of each of the bridge officer's quarters. The ensign no longer felt alone in his quarters, as he was currently in contact with T'Pol, Reed, Hoshi, and the aforementioned Trip.

The sub-commander had updated them on her impossible contact with Captain Archer hundreds of years in the future, and detailed the plan he had hatched with the help of the not-so-deceased Daniels. Now it was just a matter of getting themselves out of their locked rooms to enact the scheme.

"We could disengage the decoupling pins," Mayweather suggested, speaking into the small panel beside his door.

"It won't work," Trip's voice came over the jury-rigged com. "We can only access the pins from outside our quarters."

"So if we can't pick the locks," Mayweather replied. "What about the shafts that house the EPS conduits? They're adjacent to the air ducts."

"They were pretty much blocked off as the ship was completed," Reed chimed in through the doorbell. "They'd be too tight a squeeze."

"What's your definition of too tight?" Trip's voice asked.

"You or I couldn't get through," Reed said. "Maybe a child, or . . ."

". . . or Hoshi," Trip suggested in unison with Reed.

"It's possible," Reed said. "But it would be difficult."

"What do you say, Hoshi?" Trip asked the one silent member of the conversation. "You willing to give it a try?"

Hoshi stood in her quarters, a pale look of dread on her face. "Isn't there some other way I could help? Something that needs translating? You know how claustrophobic I am."

"There's no one else who can get through those crawlspaces," Mayweather encouraged, hoping to bypass trying to soothe her fears. "Unless we can reach Crewman Neiman. She's pretty small."

"There's no time," T'Pol interrupted the unproductive discussion. "If this is going to work, we need to begin now. Ensign Sato?"

"How far would I have to go to get to the doctor's quarters?" Hoshi asked, still concerned.

"Forty meters," T'Pol replied. "Maybe forty-five."

"Then how far to Lieutenant Reed's?" The ensign stalled while she worked up her courage.

"It's not that far, Hoshi," Trip said, trying to help calm her. "You can do it. We *need* you to do it."

Hoshi looked up at the small vent that she would have to crawl through. She had been confronting her fears every day since stepping aboard *Enterprise* ten months ago. Most of them had been conquered as new situations arose. This was just one more to deal with and she knew there really was no other option.

"Fine," she said. "But if I get stuck in there I expect you guys to tear the ship apart with your bare hands to get to me."

"We promise," Trip replied. She took a small comfort in hearing those words.

"Here I go," she said with a sigh.

Hoshi grabbed her flashlight and slid a chair beneath the vent. Since she didn't have anything slim enough to pry the grate open, she repeatedly banged the end of her flashlight against it until the metal buckled. She then grabbed the loose corner and pulled it away from the wall. The vent looked even smaller without the grate covering it. She dropped her flashlight inside before removing her uniform jacket and pulling herself up the wall.

The passageway was extremely narrow. It wasn't exactly filthy, but it certainly wasn't spit polish clean like the rest of the ship. A cooling breeze blew through the air duct, keeping Hoshi's cabin the same comfortable temperature as the entire ship. The beam from her flashlight was the only illumination in the small dark tunnel.

This is not *going to be fun,* she thought as she squeezed her way into the air duct.

Hoshi took several deep breaths as she tried to orient herself within the confined space. The metal pressed against her back and sides. The cool air was doing little to ease her rising claustrophobia. With a last calming breath she pulled her body forward on her elbows.

The air vent opened up a little as it deposited her into the shafts with the EPS conduits. But a real problem quickly arose. The smooth walls were gone, replaced by conduits of different lengths crisscrossing in every direction. Hoshi was able to move on her hands and knees, but she had to crawl over and around the conduit to continue forward. Her flashlight beam barely broke through the inky darkness.

We should install lighting in these things, she thought as she took several more deep breaths. *It's okay, Hoshi, only about twenty more meters to go.*

Hoshi had to contort her body around a section of conduit. She was sweating freely as she wondered where the cool air had gone. Maybe it didn't circulate through these shafts. Her body became more smudged with grease and dirt with the passing of each conduit. It was going to take an extremely long hot shower to make her feel clean again.

There was a noise coming from somewhere, a repetitive beat that was getting closer.

Footsteps.

She paused, then carefully leaned forward to peek through a tiny opening in the conduit housing that allowed her to look down into the corridor below. The sound she had heard was indeed footsteps. Two armed Suliban walked directly beneath her as Hoshi held her breath and remained as still as her shaking body could. She listened until she heard footsteps fade away, and then waited a few moments more.

Once she was sure that it was clear, Hoshi continued along the tight ducts carrying on a silent conversation in her head to calm her nerves.

"Maybe a small child or Hoshi" can fit inside.

Great idea.

Wait, why not Porthos? He's certainly smaller than me.

When I get out of this thing, I'm putting that damned dog through an intensive training program. And he can have all the cheese he wants!

She wiped the sweat from her brow as she fit her body through another tight passage. Her claustrophobia was beginning to overwhelm her, but she somehow managed to keep it in check. *The entire crew is counting on you,* she reminded herself as she made her way through the ducts, getting closer to Phlox's quarters.

The good doctor was sitting at his desk, humming softly while working on the project that he had been given. He had pulled a pair of hyposprays from the emergency med-kit he kept in his quarters and was busy placing a couple tiny ampules into them. The work stopped when he heard a bang from above that caused him to jump. He silently berated himself for being so tense and got up from his chair.

Phlox grabbed a small tool from his kit and pulled the chair he had been sitting on toward the center of the room and climbed up on it. He used the tool to pry off the grating of the small air vent built into his ceiling.

A hand reached through the open vent.

"Hoshi?" Phlox asked in a voice just slightly above a whisper.

"Good guess," she replied, using her sarcasm to relieve some of the tension.

"How are you holding up?" the doctor asked with serious concern for her well-being.

"Great," Hoshi lied as she braced herself within her cramped quarters. "If you don't mind, I'd like to get this over with."

Phlox handed her the hyposprays, giving her hand a little squeeze of encouragement. "Good luck."

With great difficulty, she slid her arm beneath her body. Once she got it past the rib cage, she reached for her waist and pushed the hyposprays into the back pocket of her uniform pants. Her body was twisted in an unnatural shape.

I never knew I was such a contortionist. Maybe I can join a circus. She tried to make light of her serious situation to relieve some of the pressure. It wasn't working.

It's all up from here, she thought as she pulled herself

to a junction in the shafts. For once luck was on her side. The vertical tube that led up to B-deck was wide enough for her to maneuver through. Even better, the conduit was firmly attached to the walls in such a way that she could use it like rungs on a ladder and climb up to the higher deck. It only took a few minutes before she was back in the tight embrace of another one of the horizontal ducts. This one was in the ceiling above B-deck.

Hoshi crawled along the conduits, peering through gaps in the passageway to see into the corridors below. She stopped when she recognized an intersection and made a right turn, continuing with newfound resolve. *I may not enjoy what I'm doing,* she thought, *but at least I think I know where I'm going.*

She crawled along a few feet past the intersection and found what she had been looking for. Through another gap in the conduit, she could see the door to Reed's quarters. Her final destination was only a meter away. However, that meter would require her to leave the tight confines of the conduits into the open and exposed corridor where any number of Suliban could stumble across her. *From the frying pan into the fire.*

Hoshi shined her flashlight on the conduits below her. *I am never going to make it through that tight space,* she thought. But she found strength in the combination of her overwhelming desire to get free of the claustrophobic space with the need to go on with the escape plan. Steeling her resolve, she took a deep breath and pulled her body forward.

There was still a meter between her and the ceiling grate beneath the collection of conduit. Once she had passed the opening in the pipes, Hoshi slid her legs back down into the tight hole. They had managed to fit fairly well. Now it was just a matter of sliding past her hips and upper body. As she lowered her body, her worst nightmare suddenly came true. She was stuck.

Hard metal pressed against her hips as she tried to push past it. Her shallow breaths came quickly as her panic grew. She knew that if she didn't calm herself, she would be in danger of hyperventilating.

Calm down, she ordered herself. *You can do this. It's only a matter of a meter.*

Hoshi settled her breathing and expelled one last deep breath to constrict her rib cage. She gave one final push, sliding her torso past the tight confluence of metal. Both hands clutched onto the conduit above her as she continued to lower her body. The metal suddenly felt cooler against her skin as Hoshi realized that the material of her tank top was no longer between her and the conduit.

The shirt had been snagged in the same junction of conduits that had trapped her lower body. The cloth was riding up her back as she slid lower down through the opening. She tried to brace her legs against the walls, but the opening between the conduit and ceiling grate did not give her anything to press against. The shirt rose higher as she tried to twist her body to pull it free. Hoshi knew that she would have to release one of her hands from its hold to remove the snag, but that could throw her off balance and send her crashing through the ceiling grate.

Not a very stealthy option, she thought.

The ensign paused for a second, trying to consider some logical way out of the situation, but there was only one she could think of. With a sigh of resignation, she continued to lower herself between the conduit as her shirt was torn away from her body.

Once through the mass of metals, she found her footing and peered out through the grate. The corridor below her was empty, but she could not be sure how long it would stay that way. Shirtless, she kicked her way through the grating and dropped into the hall below.

Hoshi hugged her arms against her body as she checked to confirm that no one had heard her. She was still alone. *Good thing,* she thought, *because I'd never be able to explain to the Suliban what I'm doing out of my quarters topless.* She stepped over to the door panel and worked the controls, typing in a complex series of commands to override the door lock. As Hoshi hit the final command, she covered her chest with her hands just in time to see the door to Reed's quarters open.

Reed had been pacing, and she'd caught him mid-stride. She could see by the look on his face that he was quite shocked by her appearance. Dirty, sweaty, and half-naked, Hoshi was sure she must be quite a sight.

"Whatever you're about to say," she said, stepping into the room, "I don't want to hear it. Just get me a shirt."

The lieutenant hesitated, not knowing whether to offer comfort or laugh. Once he regained his composure, he turned to his closet as Hoshi confirmed that no one was coming behind her.

"Here, try this," he said, handing her a T-shirt. "It might be a bit big."

"I'm not really picky," she replied, waiting for him to turn away.

Reed paused for a moment, then realized his faux pas and averted his eyes. "Sorry," he said, stepping into the bathroom to wet a washcloth for her. "How was it making your way through the ducts?"

"Tight," she said as she pulled the shirt over her head. "How do you and Trip get any work done in there if something needs repairs?"

"Most of the tactical systems are fairly accessible," he replied. "I don't know how the commander gets done half the things that he needs to though."

"You can look now," she said once the shirt was on. "It would be a lot more convenient if there were some kind of access way built into the wall, you know."

Reed handed her the washcloth. "That's what Commander Jefferies back at the Starfleet Design Center kept insisting while the ship was being built. He'll be pleased to hear that someone agrees with him."

"It will be the first call I make when we get back in contact with home," Hoshi said as she wiped the grime from her face. "Let's get moving."

The pair stepped back into the corridor. They wanted to

free half the crew, but knew that it was impossible to do that with all the Suliban stalking through the ship. Instead they focused on the plan and made their way to the other bridge officers on B-deck. They didn't even want to risk a ride in the turbolift to get Mayweather until they had some more support on their side.

Chapter 20

Enterprise was as quiet as a tomb, which was just how the Suliban liked it. The pair of soldiers who had returned T'Pol to her quarters were walking their endless patrol of B-deck. The job was blissfully simple with the entire *Enterprise* crew locked safely in their quarters and the soldiers had settled into a relaxed stride as they moved through the corridors.

The routine patrol suddenly changed, however, when they rounded a corner and were surprised to find the Vulcan slumped on the floor far from her quarters. She was leaning against a bulkhead, apparently still dazed from the drugs Silik had given her to help with his questioning.

The soldiers glanced at each other as they silently placed blame for having been so careless as to forget to lock her door after they had left. Obviously one of them had to have made the careless oversight for the female to have been able to get out on her own. The soldiers drew their weapons and cautiously approached in case they had actually locked the door and something else was afoot. One of the guards moved to a nearby intersection to confirm they were alone. He nodded to his partner indicating that neither *Enterprise* personnel nor Suliban officers were approaching.

"What are you doing?" the Suliban asked T'Pol.

Her head lolled to the side while her face squinted up into the light. She didn't even seem to notice they were standing above her. A soft moan escaped her lips.

"Stand up, Vulcan!" he commanded.

But she continued to ignore him, mumbling something incoherent to herself about the Vulcan Science Directorate.

"Up!" he insisted, wondering how she had managed to wander so far in this state and not be seen by one of the other patrols.

When she still refused to move, the soldier planted a swift kick into her side. There was no reaction.

He directed the other Suliban to pick her up. The soldier stepped away from the intersection and roughly grabbed her under the arms, hauling her to her feet. She began thrashing wildly, but she wasn't trying to pull away from him. It was if she had lost control of her own body. The Suliban was having trouble keeping hold of her.

His partner placed his weapon against her temple. "Stand up!" he insisted as he tried to keep the disruptor trained on her moving body.

T'Pol ignored the weapon as she continued to convulse.

The two Suliban looked at each other as if wondering what to do next. But before they could figure it out, Reed and Trip dropped down from a pair of open panels in the ceiling. The Suliban were caught off guard and injected with sedatives from the hyposprays Phlox had loaded. The guards were unconscious before they could even use their weapons, their bodies slumped to the deck.

T'Pol suddenly regained her composure and stood up by her own volition. She grabbed the hyposprays from the *Enterprise* officers and the weapons from the Suliban soldiers. She then opened the door to Trip's quarters so he and Reed could drag the unconscious bodies into the safe hiding place.

Hoshi was waiting for them in the engineer's quarters still wearing Reed's shirt. The officers deposited the Suliban inside, shoving them out of the way against the bulkhead.

"You certainly took your time," T'Pol noted as she handed Trip a weapon. "He had this pressed against my forehead."

"Had to make sure they were preoccupied," Trip replied, smiling.

T'Pol chose not to comment as she handed the other weapon to Reed.

"You positive you're willing to do this?" Trip asked the lieutenant. "It could get pretty ugly."

Reed understood the gravity of what Trip was implying. "I'm positive," he said, knowing there was no other choice and no other person on the ship he would allow to take his place.

"You've got thirty minutes," Trip said.

"Good luck," Reed said. Before anyone could wish him the same, he exited back into the corridor and made his way to the turbolift. Every part of their plan was dangerous. His was just a little more personally so.

Once Reed was safely on his way, T'Pol handed the pair of hyposprays to Hoshi. "If they regain consciousness," she said, indicating the Suliban, "don't hesitate to use these."

"Don't worry," Hoshi said, with a sense of conviction.

Trip peered out the door confirming that Reed was gone and no one else was coming. He turned back to T'Pol. "Let's go."

The pair moved out into the corridor, heading in the opposite direction as Reed. Hoshi watched as they turned a corner and were gone. She closed the door and took a seat on Trip's bunk, clutching the two hyposprays and keeping an eye on the unconscious Suliban.

Reed was on the move, cautiously making his way through the corridors of E-deck, Suliban weapon in hand. He heard footsteps as he approached an intersection and paused. There was no place to hide in the corridor he was standing in. He was too far from the turbolift and the Suliban would most certainly hear his hurried footsteps. Reed saw an escape route in the bulkhead beside him and, taking a page from Hoshi's book, pulled open a hatch in the wall.

The lieutenant squeezed himself inside the tight space and pulled the hatch shut. The door clicked softly a moment before the Suliban turned the corner. Reed listened as their footsteps moved off down the corridor. He thought he heard the *whoosh* of the turbolift doors opening and closing in the distance.

The corridor was silent once again.

Reed waited a moment and carefully reopened the hatch, peering into the corridor. It was empty. Pushing the metal away, he stepped back into the hall with a sigh of relief. If he'd been caught before he arrived at his destination their entire plan would have been blown.

The corridors were mercifully empty as he continued around the corner. He remembered back when he had made the same walk with his captain just a few days earlier, and wondered if he would ever walk the decks of the ship with Archer again. The cabin they'd gone to was just ahead; Reed could see the shining red light on the mag-lock.

Reed punched in the now familiar code and the lock disengaged with a click. The lieutenant immediately froze to listen for footsteps. It hadn't been a loud noise, but to Reed it had echoed throughout the deck. Satisfied, he removed the lock and tapped on the panel to open the door. It swung away with a hiss.

The dimly lit room looked exactly as it had the other day when he and the captain had retrieved the device with the designs for the Suliban *stealth*-cruiser. He assumed that the Suliban had given up on getting into the room when they were unable to open the lock. Their scanners would have told them that the captain was not inside, so they probably just left it alone.

Reed entered the quarters and set the mag-lock down on the nearest table. The door closed behind him, sealing him safely into the room. Once again, he found himself in the place that he knew to be a virtual treasure trove of future technology. But the temptation to explore it was muted this time. He had a very specific task to carry out.

The locker looked no different; standard Starfleet issue. The contents, however, were anything but. He opened it revealing the same garments he had seen the last time he had been in there. The T-shirt the captain had briefly removed from the top of the device they had gotten before was once again resting on a shelf. Nothing that looked out of the ordinary.

Carefully, Reed checked the inside of the locker door. It was easy to find the latch on the thin metal casing. He slid the release mechanism aside and opened a hidden compartment obviously added after the ship had left the spacedock. Reed reached his fingers into the compartment. Then his whole hand. Then part of his arm. He felt around the empty compartment, trying not to worry about where his hand actually was at the moment. The metal door was only a couple of centimeters thick, and his arm had been inserted much deeper than that.

Suddenly, he felt the device under his palm and grasped hold of it. It was slightly larger than a padd and not very heavy at all. Reed pulled it and the missing part of his arm out of the thin metal door. It was exactly where the captain had told T'Pol it would be.

With satisfaction, he closed the locker and picked up the mag-lock. He stepped back into the corridor and gently replaced the lock on the door. A sense of accomplishment overwhelmed him as he held the device. The easy part of the plan had succeeded. *Now comes the fun part,* he thought sarcastically.

As if to prove himself right, Reed turned and found a pair of Suliban soldiers standing about three meters away. Their weapons were trained directly on him. There was nowhere he could hide.

Chapter 21

Although he was sitting in the captain's chair, Reed found it difficult to sit up straight. His back ached from the blows he had taken, but he wasn't sure if that hurt any more than the ache in his gut, his ribs that were *definitely* cracked, or the pain in his jaw. There was blood coming from some part of his body, but he couldn't be sure from where. All he knew for certain was that his uniform was stained at the wrist. It was possible that the blood had soaked through from an injury to his hand or arm—or it might have gotten there when he had wiped his forehead. Now that he thought about it, his head ached as well.

Silik and Raan stood in front of him, although he couldn't tell one from the other through his bleary eyes. *I might have a concussion*. It didn't much matter, though. They looked fine. No one had beaten the bloody day-lights out of them today. *But the day's not over yet*. Reed comforted himself with that thought.

The device Reed had retrieved from Daniels's quarters was nestled in Silik's hand. The Cabal leader hadn't laid a hand on the lieutenant. That had been work for Raan and a couple of the soldiers. They seemed to enjoy their jobs.

"Did you think we wouldn't be watching Daniels's quarters?" Silik asked in a rather cocky tone for someone who let others do his dirty work.

"I guess I wasn't thinking," Reed said defiantly, wincing through the pain. He could taste a thin trickle of blood in his mouth.

"I guess you weren't," Silik smugly agreed, turning over the device. "But you should be thinking now—thinking about what will happen if you don't answer my questions." He moved in closer. "Are you thinking about that, Lieutenant Reed?"

Reed nodded reluctantly. It hurt too much for him to come up with an appropriately smug response.

"Good," Silik said as he held the device out to the lieutenant. "Now tell me what this is? What does it do?"

"I don't know."

Raan stepped up and delivered a fierce backhand punch across Reed's jaw. The pain was excruciating. The bridge faded from view for a moment as Reed came close to blacking out.

"What does it do?" Silik insisted.

The battered lieutenant was having trouble speaking. Blood was flowing freely in his mouth now. "I don't know."

Raan moved to strike again, but Reed shied away, covering his face.

"Please!" he begged.

Silik placed a hand out, stopping Raan. He leaned into his prisoner again. "Yes?" he asked with anticipation.

"I'm supposed to destroy it," Reed said, looking as if he was trying to keep from breaking down entirely. "I don't know what it does."

Silik smiled. Anything the *Enterprise* crew wanted destroyed was definitely something his benefactor would love to get his hands on. "Who told you to destroy it?" the Suliban asked.

Reed hesitated for a moment, forcing Raan to step forward again. The commander raised his hand menacingly.

"Captain Archer," Reed spat out with a little blood. "Before he left. He didn't want you to find it."

Silik was even more intrigued. This was an unexpected surprise indeed. "And why would that be?" he asked.

"He said you would use it," Reed explained, haltingly. "To contact someone. I don't know who. I swear."

The smile returned to Silik's face. "Have the lieutenant returned to his quarters," he ordered Raan. He looked down at the device, knowing that he had what he needed, and headed for the turbolift.

The atmosphere in engineering was far more sedate than that on the bridge. A trio of Suliban soldiers was stationed in the room. Two of them stood watch at alternate sides of the warp engine. The third was on the platform maintaining the warp controls and learning whatever he could about the mechanics of the Earth vessel. The technology was slightly less advanced than what the Suliban possessed—and had been given—but there were a few elements to the engine that the soldier hadn't seen before.

Suddenly the blast of a Suliban weapon cut through the stillness of the room, striking one of the two guards on the deck. As he fell to the ground, the other two Suliban drew their weapons and began firing toward the upper level in the direction from which the blast had originated. Before they could isolate their target, another blast knocked one of the soldiers off his feet.

The remaining Suliban saw Commander Tucker taking refuge behind a support beam. The soldier took cover while looking for a clear shot. He could see a good portion of the commander's body from his angle on the ground and he took aim. As he prepared to fire, a hand snaked out from behind him and pinched him between the shoulder and neck. He fell to the floor unconscious.

Once she confirmed the Suliban would not be getting up any time soon, T'Pol moved to a nearby panel. Trip slid down the ladder from the upper deck of engineering to join her on the main level.

"Ready?" she asked.

Trip jumped onto the platform and pushed one of the unconscious Suliban aside. He worked quickly at the controls, knowing it would not be long before someone came to look in on them.

Silik left *Enterprise* in Raan's capable hands and took the futuristic device with him back to the Helix. He placed it on the circular platform in the temporal chamber, hoping to reestablish contact with his mysterious benefactor from the future. The controls on the instrument were foreign to him and he was having a difficult time activating it. But just when he began to believe his efforts were futile, a single light on the device started to blink, and it began to emit a low hum.

His face became animated with anticipation. He was finally going to make contact. Although he still did not have Archer, he hoped that the technology he now possessed was more valuable.

"Hello?" he asked, looking up at the platform. "Are you there?"

There was no response.

"I have wonderful news," Silik announced into the air. "Technology from your future."

Silik waited but nothing happened. He turned his attention back to the device. He had done something right; now it was just a matter of building on his success and getting the instrument fully operational.

The loud Klaxon of an alarm sounded on the *Enterprise* bridge. Raan and the Suliban crew reacted to the unknown warning, checking their monitors for some kind of indication of what it meant. One of the soldiers called Raan over to the engineering station and pointed to the console. The commander looked over the information, unwilling to believe what it said.

He tapped a companel with extreme urgency. "Engineering," he called into the air. "How did this happen?"

But engineering did not respond.

"Engineering?" he called again.

Silence.

Raan turned his gaze to the soldiers posted by the turbolift. They immediately understood the unspoken command and stepped to the lift to check the situation out. As they headed for engineering, Raan tried to do what he could using the bridge controls, having little hope that anything would work. Giving up, he reached for his communications device to get in touch with the Helix.

Silik leaned over the future device, intently working at the unfamiliar controls. Three lights were blinking now, although there was no other indication that he was making any kind of progress. A beeping sound broke through the silence, but the excitement it brought was dashed when Silik realized the noise was coming from a nearby station. He reluctantly left the device for a moment.

"What is it?" he said, tapping the companel with annoyance.

"The antimatter stream has been compromised," Raan urgently reported from the *Enterprise* bridge.

"Shut down the warp reactor," Silik replied with the obvious response. He wondered why Raan had bothered him with such a simple problem to solve.

"Our people in engineering aren't responding," Raan reported. "I've sent soldiers."

"Keep me informed," Silik said as he terminated contact.

He knew that he should return to *Enterprise*. If they lost Archer *and* his ship, Silik wasn't sure that any amount of technology would make up for it in the eyes of his benefactor. But the device drew his attention away. Once he made contact he would receive his long delayed instructions. For all he knew the plans could have changed and the mysterious figure could now want *Enterprise* destroyed whether or not the Suliban delivered Archer to him.

Engineering was in chaos with sirens wailing and steam venting from the warp reactor. The Suliban soldiers sent from the bridge rushed into the room to find their fallen comrades slowly regaining consciousness beside the sparking consoles. The few monitors still active flashed urgent warnings of a reactor overload.

The soldiers ignored their colleagues as they rushed to the control panel on the raised engineering platform. The technology was unfamilar to them. But even if they had known what they were doing it would have been pointless. They desperately worked at the panel but the controls refused to respond. A small explosion at the far end of the room caused them to abandon their hopeless mission and exit to the corridor without bothering to make sure the others were following.

Success. A golden glow was emanating from the instrument and rising about a foot into the air. It did not yet match the intensity of the shaft of light the benefactor figure usually stood in, but Silik assumed it was only a matter of time. As excitement rose, so too did his level of irritation when another interruption from the companel broke his concentration.

"Yes?" he snapped into the com.

"These humans are greater fools than I thought," Raan's voice came back at him. "They'd rather commit mass suicide than submit to us."

Silik needed to get back to the device. "Did you correct the problem?" he impatiently asked.

"It's too late," Raan said. "The reactor's going to breach."

Silik considered his options and realized that he was only going to have the device to present to his benefactor. "We can't endanger the Helix," he simply replied. "Evacuate, and have *Enterprise* towed out of the nebula."

"There's very little time," Raan replied with increasing urgency. "Will you alert the tractor teams?"

You've got an entire complement of soldiers, was all Silik could think. "You do it," he replied, looking back at the waiting device. "I'm busy."

Again he terminated the communication and returned to the golden glow.

"Where are you?" he asked aloud.

216

* * *

Raan sounded the alarm to evacuate ship. With all the other warnings blaring throughout *Enterprise,* he worried that all of his crew might not make it. *Of course, the pitiful human crew must be even the more concerned by the alarms.* The idea brought a smile to his face as he hurried for the nearest docking port.

The ship was trembling as Raan hurried through the halls past closed doors of worried crewmen. He could hear the sounds of distant explosions as he reached the airlock and found most of his men filing through the doors. It was likely that the same evacuation procedure was taking place at the other docking ports on the ship. Their quick evacuation was as much of a credit to their training as it was a personal goal of self-preservation. Once Raan confirmed that the cell-ship was fully loaded, he closed the airlock, literally sealing the fate of the *Enterprise* crew.

Good-bye, Enterprise, he thought as he watched the ship slowly fade into the nebula.

Two cell-ships passed Raan's fleeing vessel. He watched as the green tractor beams shot out at *Enterprise* and the ships began the process of towing it away from the Helix. The beams had locked onto the saucer and allowed them to move it at a good clip. Plumes of plasma exhaust were trailing from both of the nacelles. He could imagine the sounds of destruction being absorbed by the vacuum of space.

* * *

The golden glow of the mysterious device had changed into a hazy column of yellow light. Silik sat mesmerized by the beam waiting for it to take a more solid form. He stood back about a dozen feet preparing to make contact and report on his new find.

A darkened shape slowly began to form within the glow. Silik's eyes widened with anticipation as the figure began to take on a humanoid shadow.

"Is that you?" he asked with excited anticipation. "Can you hear me?"

No response.

The shape continued to form.

The cell-ships emerged from the nebula towing *Enterprise* to a safe distance. Arcs of crackling blue and white energy jumped between the Starfleet ship's nacelles. Plasma was now flowing freely from the ship, leaving a pair of trails behind that cut through the darkness of space. The arcing energy increased in intensity as small explosions occurred at points of impact on the ship's exterior. Small scorch marks were forming on the hull as a prelude to its imminent destruction.

The cell-ships disengaged their tractor beams and quickly moved away from *Enterprise*. The crews obviously did not want to get caught in the ship's demise. The arcs of energy cracked more wildly then before and the explosions rocked the ship.

One of the plumes of plasma ignited in a spectacular flash. It sent out an immense wave of gaseous flames toward one of the Suliban ships. The pilot of the cell-ship frantically worked the controls to get himself out of the line of fire and impending explosion. His tiny cockpit was illuminated by the fireworks.

The two cell-ships rolled back to the nebula trying to put as much distance between themselves and *Enterprise* as they could. The Suliban looked back as the ship faded from view and pitied the poor souls trapped on board.

As the Suliban ships disappeared behind the red veil, the arcs of energy surrounding *Enterprise* diminished and the explosions on its outer hull sputtered out. The plumes of plasma exhaust were last to disappear, but soon even they were slowly fading into space.

After a brief moment, the two nacelles flared with power. *Enterprise* lurched forward, but rather than exploding, it jumped to warp, escaping Suliban territory.

On the bridge, T'Pol was in the captain's chair with most of the crew in their usual positions monitoring consoles and performing their duties. Reed, however, was down in sickbay, recovering from the brutal beating he had taken at the hands of their captors.

"The antimatter stream is back to normal," Mayweather reported from his station.

"You may have overdone your pyrotechnic display," T'Pol said to Trip as she confirmed the information from her own screen on the arm of the chair. "The scorching on the starboard nacelle is extensive."

"I'll try to remember that the next time we have to fake

a reactor breach," Trip responded with his typical brand of sarcasm laced with Southern charm.

An alarm started beeping—just one of the many alarms the ship had sounded in the past hour.

"Cell-ships! Thirty of them," Hoshi anxiously announced from her station. She had managed to replace her uniform, but had not had enough time to take that hot shower. "Thirty-five! Approaching at high warp."

"Maintain your course and speed, ensign," T'Pol ordered Mayweather calmly.

Mayweather, however, shared Hoshi's concern.

Silik continued to watch the evolving shape within the glowing column of light. It had definitely taken on the form of a humanoid figure. But the mysterious being had yet to respond to him.

"I've tried to reach you," Silik explained, hoping that he would not be punished. "I've tried for two days." All the excitement he had felt about making contact had shifted to fear. "I did what you told me but Archer wasn't aboard *Enterprise*. There was some kind of temporal signature. I need instructions!"

The figure continued to stand motionless in the light. There was no response.

"I don't know how to operate this device," Silik pleaded. "I need your help!"

Finally the figure spoke—but its voice was severely distorted and completely unintelligible. To Silik it was a gift. He had made contact.

"I hear you, but I don't understand," he said with equal amounts of excitement and trepidation. "Repeat what you said. Please repeat what you said."

There was an interminable moment of silence as Silik waited for the words to come again. He noticed movement within the light and assumed that his benefactor was trying to break through the centuries to relay his instructions. Silik was practically shaking with excitement. He was not going to be punished. He might even be rewarded. All he could think about were the new and exciting gifts that he was about to receive.

The figure shifted on the platform and then suddenly leaped forward through the column of light. He exploded into the reality of the temporal chamber. His body took on solid form with a most definitely human appearance, as it jumped off the platform.

"I said, 'You're an ugly bastard.'" Captain Archer tackled the Suliban and the two men landed hard on the floor and rolled across the deck. Silik quickly overcame his astonishment enough to fight back, but Archer had already used the element of surprise to his advantage. He gained the upper hand before the Suliban could think to use any of his genetic tricks.

Silik threw a punch at Archer, but his fist hardly connected. Without hesitation, Archer brought up his own hand. He was holding an object that Silik couldn't make out. Archer didn't give the Suliban time to react as he brought the hand down hard on Silik's face.

Archer released the item from his hand. It was the piece

of concrete he had used to pound out the copper wire. It rolled across the deck while Silik lay dazed from its impact. Archer reached into the Suliban's holster and removed his weapon. He placed it against Silik's temple as his prisoner stirred to consciousness.

"If you try shape-shifting on me," Archer said, pressing the weapon into the mottled green yellow skin, "or pulling one of your chameleon routines, I promise you, Silik, I'll blow your head off."

Chapter 22

"Has *Enterprise* left the nebula?" Archer asked, still holding the weapon on Silik.

"Can't you see? I've brought you Archer!" Silik called out to his benefactor in a last desperate attempt to vindicate himself. "He's here! Archer's here! There's no need to punish me!"

"Where's my ship, Silik?" Archer insisted.

It finally started to dawn on the Cabal leader that he was alone. "They've left," he said. "They're gone."

"How many cell-ships did you send after them?" Archer asked.

But Silik's mind was too preoccupied to respond.

"Silik!" Archer persisted.

"I don't know," Silik answered honestly. He'd turned the mission over to Raan, and could only guess. "Twenty? Thirty?"

"You're going to call them off," Archer said, then remembered something that T'Pol had told him. "And then you're going to give me back those data discs. Now get up, nice and slowly."

"My soldiers won't let you leave," Silik defiantly stated.

"Get up," Archer demanded.

Silik reluctantly rose to his feet. Archer pushed him toward the exit, but stopped before they crossed the threshold. The captain held tightly to his prisoner as he removed the weapon from Silik's forehead. Archer slowly turned back into the room and took aim. It only took a single blast to obliterate the device sitting on the platform.

Enterprise raced through space with a pack of cell-ships on its tail. Hopelessly outgunned, the Starfleet vessel returned fire as it fled.

Sickbay shuddered under the assault and Phlox's critter collection let loose with a series of howls and chattering. The doctor alternated between calming the animals and tending to one disagreeable patient.

"I need to get to the bridge," Reed insisted as he sat up on the biobed, taking a moment to steady himself.

"No, Lieutenant, you don't," Phlox replied as he attempted to gently guide Reed back down on the bed. "I'm not happy with the looks of that concussion. I don't need you injuring yourself again by slamming yourself into a console."

"If the ship is destroyed it won't very well matter what

happens to my head," Reed replied caustically. He tried to stand but fell back onto the bed. A moment later the ship trembled again. If he had only waited a second he could have blamed his fall on the jolt.

"And if you can hardly stand you can hardly expect to be able aim the ship's weapons can you?" the doctor shot back with a menacing look. The amiable doctor with the impossibly large smile Reed was used to was gone.

A pain shot through Reed's head. He knew the doctor was right but it didn't make it any easier. He had been trapped in his quarters while Suliban took control of the ship and now he was stuck in sickbay during a relentless attack. He didn't care that he had sacrificed his own body in their scheme to retrieve the captain. He didn't even know if that sacrifice had been worthwhile—was the captain back? And he couldn't believe that he had taken a brutal beating from the Suliban and yet couldn't manage to defy one generally easygoing Denobulan doctor.

The ship shook once more as it came under fire.

I need to be at my station, Reed thought as he reluctantly lay back on the bed.

"Hoshi? Any sign of the Vulcan ship?" Trip asked in desperation.

"Not yet!" she yelled over the din. There was nothing on her monitor except for the thirty-five Suliban ships.

Enterprise rocked with a hard shake as consoles exploded around the bridge.

"Hull plating on the port-aft quarter's offline!" Mayweather reported.

Another jolt shook the ship.

"Alter course," T'Pol commanded. "Ten degrees starboard."

Mayweather slowly turned the ship as T'Pol had ordered. He was angling its vulnerable port quarter away from the pursuing cell-ships so the less damaged sections of hull could absorb the repeated impact of the Suliban weapons.

Tensions were rising on the bridge as the siege continued.

"They're closing!" Mayweather yelled.

Trip frantically worked the tactical controls and the aft phase cannon let loose a powerful beam. It struck a cell-ship, which tumbled out of control and smashed into another vessel. Both enemy vessels were destroyed.

"The lead ships are overtaking us," Hoshi reported with barely concealed fear.

A massive jolt struck *Enterprise* as the crew held onto whatever they could to keep from flying across the bridge.

The attacking cell-ships continued to blaze around *Enterprise*. They were pummeling the ship with weapons fire in what seemed remarkably like a space-based version of a bee swarm attacking.

"Port hull-plating's down!" Mayweather reported, with fear beginning to creep into his own voice. "Ventral plating as well."

Several blasts resounded across the bridge and then . . .

everything suddenly went silent. There was a long quiet beat.

For a moment, Hoshi thought she had died. "Why did they stop firing?" she asked as she checked her monitor.

"Why waste ammunition?" Mayweather responded with a sense of defeat. "They have us surrounded."

The swarm of cell-ships encircling *Enterprise* hung in space. None of the ships made a move toward the Starfleet vessel. The Suliban did not try to initiate contact.

The silence continued on the *Enterprise* bridge as the crew tried to figure out what was going on.

"Are long range sensors still operational?" T'Pol asked.

Hoshi gave a somber nod. "No Vulcan ship," she replied.

And then the bridge monitors displayed a truly astonishing sight. The cell-ships were starting to peel away from *Enterprise* one by one. They were retreating from their prey as if they were the ones in danger.

Mayweather studied his console, confused. "Sub-Commander?"

"I see them," T'Pol responded, confirming the scans on the armchair console.

"Son of a bitch!" Trip rejoiced as he watched the last few cell-ships disappear from his screen. "He did it!"

An alarm sounded at Mayweather's station.

"One cell-ship," he reported with a smile. "Approaching from aft."

"Stand down weapons," T'Pol commanded Trip solely

for the sake of formality. She then turned to Hoshi. "Open a channel."

Hoshi worked at her station, then nodded to T'Pol.

"*Enterprise* to Suliban vessel," T'Pol said.

"Go ahead, *Enterprise*," Captain Archer's welcome voice came over the com.

Smiles from the entire crew, save the Vulcan, spread across the bridge.

"Good to hear your voice, Captain," Trip spoke for them all.

"Good to hear yours," Archer agreed from behind the controls of the Suliban ship. "I feel like I've been away for a thousand years. Is everyone all right?"

"Lieutenant Reed suffered some minor injuries," T'Pol reported. "But he's recovering in sickbay."

Archer was pleased to hear that his crew had gotten through the experience mostly intact. Although he could see that his ship had suffered a fair amount of damage.

"Captain, I'm curious," T'Pol added over the com. "Why didn't the other cell-ships try to stop you?"

"I know it's not standard Starfleet procedure, but I took a hostage," Archer admitted as he looked down to confirm that Silik was still unconscious at his feet. "By the time he wakes up, we'll be long gone."

Archer had considered taking the Suliban prisoner with them as he was responsible for the deaths of the Paraagan colonists. But the captain knew they had only gotten a brief reprieve from the cell-ships. If they held on to Silik, he expected that the Suliban would stop at nothing to retrieve their leader, even if it meant killing him in the process. Archer knew that he and Silik would have their day again some time in the future.

"Request permission to dock," Archer lightly asked.

"Permission granted," T'Pol replied, finally allowing almost the smallest hint of a smile as her lips curled up slightly at the edges.

Chapter 23

A day later, the crew had managed to clean up and heal some wounds. Repairs to the ship had begun, but it was going to take a while to get everything back in ship-shape. Trip's faked warp core breach was a little closer to the real thing than anyone would have hoped. Of course, they still had to learn whether or not they really needed to bother with the repairs at all.

Enterprise had docked with the Vulcan ship, *D'kyr,* only a short time ago. The conversation between Archer and her captain had been brief and more clipped than the usual human and Vulcan interactions. T'Pol seemed to be avoiding her compatriots altogether, which led Archer to believe that there was something going on with the sub-commander of which he was unaware.

The two *D'kyr* officers had joined the senior staff on the *Enterprise* bridge. They were all standing stiffly at attention, watching the viewscreen. Both Vulcans and humans were in dress uniforms. The atmosphere was formal and tense.

The image projected before them originated on Earth and was carried through the communications satellites *Enterprise* had previously deployed, Echo One and Echo Two. Onscreen was Admiral Forrest, Commander Williams, and two other high-ranking members of the Command Council. They, too, were in dress uniforms. Ambassador Soval was also in attendance with his own Vulcan dignitaries. The meeting that took place over light-years was one of the most important in Earth's recent history.

Archer couldn't help but think that, based on what he had seen in the future, they were about to determine no less than the fate of humanity. It was a daunting task to convince the Command Council of the events of the previous few days. He stuck mainly to the facts surrounding the events in retrieving the data discs that proved their innocence in the tragedy at the Paraagan colony. A previous hurried conversation with Admiral Forrest had led them both to agree to only briefly touch on the whole notion of time travel with the Vulcans. That was a subject for conversation at a much later date.

After the captain had stated his case, the members of the Command Council made only a few comments, apparently preferring to discuss the incident in private. They did agree that there was much to consider. Even if *Enterprise* had proven the crew's innocence in the eyes of Starfleet Command, other factors would most certainly come into play. And everyone knew that "other factors" meant the

Vulcans. But with that part out of the way, Forrest turned the tribunal over to the Ambassador Soval.

Soval took a moment to consider all that he had been told. "While your explanation of how you obtained the discs is somewhat implausible," he said, "it's obvious that *Enterprise* was not responsible for the destruction of the colony."

Archer nearly broke out with a victorious cheer at finally getting through to the Vulcans. He settled for just a slight hint of a smile. "It may seem implausible to you, but . . ."

"Please allow me to finish," the ambassador interrupted.

Archer tried not to let his annoyance show. *I should have known we wouldn't get off that easily,* he thought as his body stiffened, preparing himself for Soval to continue.

"In less than a single Earth year," the ambassador said, "you've engaged in armed conflicts with over a dozen species. You've escalated the conflict between my people and the Andorians, which included the destruction of one of our most sacred monasteries. You helped eighty-nine Suliban escape from detention."

Soval paused for a moment to let the accusations hang in the air. Archer was tempted to interrupt again and explain himself, but he knew it would be pointless. Soval was gearing up for something and was not going to be swayed.

"*You* may claim to be on a mission of exploration," the ambassador continued. "I, however, consider you reckless and irresponsible—a danger to the quadrant." He turned to Admiral Forrest. "Regardless of the evidence presented here, I plan to advise the Vulcan High Command *not* to change its recommendation to Starfleet. *Enterprise* should be recalled."

The bridge crew did its best not to react. However, Trip could not contain himself. "You guys have wanted to scrub this mission from day one!" he accused. "We prove to you that we didn't kill thirty-six hundred people, but you don't want to hear it! You're pathetic!"

Archer shot him a look. This wasn't the time or the place. Although Archer certainly couldn't disagree with a thing his friend had said.

"That's enough, Commander," Forrest admonished Trip, despite the fact that he too agreed with the sentiment. Turning back to the captain, he said, "No one is more pleased than I am that *Enterprise* wasn't responsible for the tragedy, but Ambassador Soval's argument may be valid." This was the hardest part of the job for Forrest—remaining neutral. "Starfleet Command has a difficult decision to make here."

Archer knew it was his turn to speak—to defend the actions of his crew. He suspected that nothing he could say would alter the Vulcans' perception of *Enterprise*'s accomplishments, or lack thereof. However, Archer knew he wasn't just answering the Vulcans, he was convincing his own people as well.

"When I was in my early twenties on a trip to East Africa," he began, "I saw a gazelle giving birth. It was truly amazing. Within minutes the baby was standing up—standing up on its own. A few minutes more and it was walking. And before I knew it, it was running alongside its mother, moving away from the herd. Humans aren't like that, Ambassador. We may come from the same planet as those gazelles, but we're pretty much helpless when we are born. It takes us months before we're able to crawl—almost a full year before we can walk. Our deep space mission isn't much different. We're going to stumble and make mistakes. I'm sure more than a few before we find our footing. But we're going to learn from those mistakes. That's what being human's all about. I'm sorry you can't see that."

There was a quiet moment as everyone absorbed the captain's words.

"Your analogy is very colorful, Captain," Soval said with arrogance typical of his personality. "But I question whether it addresses the consequences of your actions."

Leave it to the Vulcan to miss the point entirely, Archer thought. *How am I going to convince any member of that stoic race to make an emotional decision?*

To everyone's surprise—including Archer's—a Vulcan took that moment to step forward. All eyes were on T'Pol as she seemed to be bracing herself for what she was about to say.

"The concept of learning from one's mistakes shouldn't be difficult for a Vulcan of your wisdom to understand, Ambassador," she said with a balance of respect and indictment. "Our ancestors discovered how to suppress their volatile emotions only after centuries of savage conflict. You spoke of the destruction of the monastery. What about the Vulcan listening post Captain Archer found there? I would hope our people have learned from those events that using a sacred sanctuary to spy on others was a dishonorable practice, to say the least." T'Pol paused for a moment to let the full weight of her comment sink in. "I don't wish to contradict Captain Archer, but 'learning from one's mistakes' is hardly exclusive to humans."

She exchanged a brief glance with the captain.

I think we've come pretty far in under one year, Archer thought to himself with a barely perceptible smile. He tried to lend her his strength from across the room.

"Their mission should be allowed to continue," she quietly added, doing the unthinkable in contradicting the ambassador's decision.

Soval and the other Vulcan dignitaries stood for a long silent beat. Then, without a word, they exited the conference room. The Vulcans on board *Enterprise* took the ambassador's lead and made their way onto the turbolift to return to their ship.

"The Command Council will review the evidence," Forrest said with a glance at T'Pol, "and listen to what's been said here today. I'm sure they'll hear from the Vulcans as well. I'll let you know as soon as there's a decision. Good luck, Jonathan—all of you."

Forrest tapped a button and the viewscreen switched to an image of the stars. Archer turned to his crew with a glance that told them he was appreciative of their support. He finally settled on T'Pol with a combination of shock and pride in his eyes. She met his stare and the two shared a silent moment that almost bordered on emotion.

"Hoshi, is the com still open to the rest of the ship?" he asked.

"Yes, sir," she replied. "The crew can still hear us."

"Attention all hands," he announced into the air. "It looks like our fate is now in the hands of the Command Council. I don't know what the final outcome will be, but I can tell you that I have never been more proud of any group of people I have ever worked with. If we are recalled to Earth, we will return with our heads held high. No matter what others may think, we have done a spectacular job out here, often against impressive odds. But I don't think we're going home just yet. Ambassador Soval may have listed some of our more questionable actions, but our accomplishments are many. Yes, we freed eighty-nine Suliban from a Tandaran detention center. But even in the light of recent events, I still believe those men, women, and children should be free and that the universe just might be a little better for it.

"But we can't save everyone." Archer reigned in his pride and turned it to solemnity. "We've been very busy over the past few days trying to prove our innocence. Naturally, in our quest to find the truth we had to push past the horrific events that took place at the Paraagan colony. It's always a strange thing to mourn the loss of a people you have never met. There's no shared memories—no close connections. But I know those deaths have affected every member of this crew. And I ask you to join me in a moment of silence to remember."

The bridge crew stood at their posts with heads bowed. Archer knew that the same was being done all over the ship.

T'Pol had handled all of the arrangements for their visit to the colony. He had not even spoken with any of the Paraagans and yet he felt a responsibility to each and every one of them. They had been used as nothing more than pawns in this Temporal Cold War. The people playing their games hundred of years in the future had not even cared about the colonists in the least.

Archer kept repeating one thought over in his mind as the moment of silence continued. *How many people need to die before it's no longer a "Cold War?"*

Hours later, Archer clicked off the monitor in his quarters. To say he was happy was an understatement. He roused Porthos from his rest by giving the dog a joyous rub behind the ears and received his own licks in appreciation for the attention. The hour was late, but Archer could not stay contained in his quarters.

On the way to the turbolift, Archer received an odd look from the crewmembers he passed. The captain assumed that it had something to do with the fact that he was walking around the ship wearing a robe and bedtime attire. He had been too eager to share his news to bother with putting on his uniform. Archer smiled as he stepped into the turbolift on his way to B-deck to see T'Pol.

The sub-commander had been asleep in her quarters for hours. The room was completely dark, which helped her achieve her meditative sleep. The door chime slowly roused her into the waking world. Another chime pulled her up into the sitting position.

"Come in," she called out.

The door opened, letting in the light from the corridor and a man in shadow. T'Pol hit the control and brought the room to a dim illumination. Her eyes continued to adjust to find Captain Archer standing in the doorway, dressed in his pajamas and a robe.

"I can't be sure," he said with mock concern looking back into the hall, "but Crewman Fuller might've seen me coming in here."

"She tends to be discreet," T'Pol said, surprisingly playing along. "What can I do for you?"

Archer sat beside her on the bed. "I think you put it over the top."

The puzzled look on her face had as much to do with the fact that she didn't understand the colloquialism as much as the subject matter of their conversation.

"Forrest said none of them could believe it when you went to bat for us," he said. "Not to mention the little listening post lecture you gave to Soval."

T'Pol was beginning to realize what he was talking about, in spite of her sleepiness and the captain's exuberance. "You spoke to Admiral Forrest?"

"He woke me up in the middle of the night," he replied with feigned annoyance. "Can you believe that?"

"I assume with good news."

"I think you put it over the top," he quietly repeated.

There was a definite moment between them as T'Pol realized their mission together would continue. Her evening meditation had been to help her accept the fact that she had gone against the wishes of her superiors. Although she was well aware that the end result did not really provide justification for her actions, it did help her find a bit of contentment.

Archer was fairly sure he understood the conflict going on in T'Pol's mind. He decided it would be best to leave her to her thoughts. With a nod of appreciation, he got up and went for the door.

"I still don't believe in time travel," T'Pol announced.

Archer couldn't help but smile. "The hell you don't."

Epilogue

Admiral Forrest stared at the blank screen. For the first time in days, he had actually enjoyed a conversation with another member of Starfleet. Captain Archer took the news pretty much as the admiral had expected. It was the same way he felt when he had heard the vote on the Command Council's final decision. Now, if he could only manage to get rid of the damn headache, his day would be perfect.

Forrest looked down at his desk. The piles of work had managed to accumulate over the past few days while he had to focus on the possibility of recalling *Enterprise*. He was happy that the rest of Starfleet had been moving forward and generating work as if everything was going ahead even though it meant even more for him to do once things got back to normal. He picked at the top of the pile, not quite ready to move past his current feeling of euphoria to deal with whatever the next problem was to arise.

It will all be here tomorrow, he reminded himself as he

pushed back his chair and slid out from his desk. He stood and stretched, refusing to look at the time. He knew it was late when he had contacted Archer and interrupted the captain's sleepless night. But Archer wouldn't have wanted him to wait for a more reasonable hour to make that call.

The admiral stepped out of his office to find his aide busily working at the monitor on his desk. It wasn't a surprise. Forrest knew the kid would be there. He always was.

"You know, you don't always have to wait for me to leave before you go home," Forrest said with a smile.

The aide just stared at him.

"Okay, fine," Forrest added, giving up. "I have to at least say it every now and then or else people are going to think I'm running you ragged with my demands."

"Actually, sir, people already think that no matter what you say," the aide said before he realized the words had actually come out of his mouth. His eyes bugged out in horror as he stood at attention so quickly he knocked over his chair. "Sir . . . I meant . . . I mean . . ."

"It's okay, lieutenant," the admiral said, laughing. "There may be hope for you yet."

"I'm sorry, sir," the kid insisted.

"Apology accepted," Forrest replied, standing at attention. "As you were."

"Yes, sir," the aide said, although his posture did not shift in the least.

"I'm leaving," he said. "Go home to your family."

"Soon, sir."

"How is your baby, by the way?"

A relaxed smile finally crossed the aide's face. It was the first genuine look of contentment he had seen on the lieutenant's face since he had met the kid. "He's getting bigger every day, sir," he replied.

"Well, you should spend more time with him," the admiral noted as he looked down at the digital image of the child that was kept on his aide's deck. "Put in a request for some time off."

"Yes, sir."

"Good night."

"Night, sir."

Forrest walked out of Starfleet Headquarters thinking about the lieutenant's young child. He wondered who the boy would grow into. *Would the child join Starfleet? Would Starfleet exist by the time the boy was of age?* Then he wondered more along the grander scheme of things like if the infant's descendents would be soldiers in this Temporal Cold War that Archer had spoke of.

Who could this Daniels be a descendent of? Is he even human?

Forrest knew when he lectured the cadets on making history with every step they take into space that he wasn't just blowing hot air. But Archer's recent experience made him realize the full impact of what they were doing for the first time. Even the minor decisions he made every day were leading to the unknown future.

Is the future already set? Forrest wondered. *Will we make a seemingly harmless mistake that could result in changing all that has been predetermined? How do we proceed worry-*

ing about hundreds of years of history that haven't been written yet?

Forrest's headache was intensifying. These were the kind of thoughts that would keep him from sleeping for the rest of his life. In the end, he knew that he couldn't worry about the future. He needed to concern himself with the present. *Enterprise* would continue to make strides every day. Reports would continue to come in, decisions would need to be made. One day all the decisions would lead to something bigger and better than they had even imagined. And he would oversee it all from behind his desk at Starfleet Headquarters.

ACKNOWLEDGMENTS

Special thanks to everyone at *Star Trek,* Viacom Consumer Products, and Pocket Books, especially Rick Berman, Brannon Braga, Margaret Clark, Donna O'Neill, Paula Block, and the cast and crew of *Enterprise.*